THIS IS THE END

ERIC POLLARINE

THANK YOU

First I want to thank you, the reader, for picking up this book or for downloading it, stealing it or however else you've managed to get ahold of it.

Without you, I would simply be an over-caffienated, cranky old man rambling in a Denny's, waiting for my never-ending pancakes. Thank you.

I also have to acknowledge, though it deserves much more than that, the contributions of those fighting for free speech during the present: the EFF, ACLU, Bradley Manning, WikiLeaks, Anonymous, Global Voices Online, the protesters and students that have ushered in "The Arab Spring," and Cryptome. Countless other names and groups could be typed out with countless examples of how and who have been on the frontlines of the new fight for information and speech.

My next book, *One Fine Day*, will have much longer forward and thank you sections, but I wanted those who read this to know: I appreciate what you have done. Maybe not the means, but certainly the meaning behind them.

As always, there are many people that I need to thank, but the only one that deserves my constant thanks is Angela. Though this book is my baby, if you weren't there to encourage me, I would never get anything done. I love you.

FORWARD

When I started writing *This Is The End*, I had just had my first real story accepted, just finished writing and editing "**A Man of Letters**," and I was flush full of good ideas. But as I look back now, after finally editing and formatting the final product, getting the cover ready and getting it ready for print, well, I can't help but think that maybe I jumped the gun a bit on this project.

Yeah, sure, it's ambitious to self-publish your first official book-length piece and, yeah, I did it without knowing exactly what the hell I was getting into: late nights, early mornings, videos, trailers, and sleepless nights fretting over the possibility of this thing turning into a huge flop. But was it all worth it, I have to ask myself; was doing this book without any help really the best way it could have been done?

My answer is a resounding yes. This is my little baby, my own voice, my own way of saying to the world that, yes, I am a writer and this is what I have to say. This book is my truth to power and, as I referenced it in the text, my "The Stranger." Now, don't get me wrong, this isn't to say that if I were the giving advice sort of guy, I am suggesting all writers do this, and that all writers should have complete control over their babies. I have loved working with the publishers that have generously decided to put out my previous material. But, for me, personally, *This Is The End* was too dear a piece of work to let go of. I shopped it and I am pretty sure that, even with the rough text, I could have gotten it into the hands of a publisher, but I didn't want to hassle over the cover, the layout, the QR codes, the front illustration and the T-shirts that had already been printed, so that was all out of the question. I wanted this one to be in my hands alone. I wanted its success or failure to be mine; I wanted to own this one, totally.

ERIC POLLARINE

And so here it is, finally, in all its glory, or assumed glory.
My story of Jeff and Kel and Scott. My story of life and pain
and, oh yes, of course, zombies. Though hardcore zombie
fanatics will most likely tell me that this isn't a pure zombie
novel, and I am almost half-tempted to agree with them on that.
But I think that if they or you give this book a chance, then it
will stand as a great zombie novel. Because in the end, when the
makeup and effects, blood and bone are all done being what they
are, the real appeal of Romero's true original *Night of the Living
Dead*, was the story of Ben, Barbara, Johnny and all the rest. It
was a human story, a story of suffering, pain, hope and defeat. It
was a story of the end. Just like this one.

Eric Pollarine
August 1, 2011

THIS IS THE END

PART ONE

1.

"Are you sure?" I ask him again.

I'm looking right at the motherfucker, right into his face, right into his big asshole brown eyes and he can't even bear to look back at me. He can't justify the answer that he's given me, even if I just spent, literally, well over two million dollars for him and his "crack team" of doctors to triple-check the results of the first test.

"I'm quite sure, Mr. Sorbenstein, that it's cancer."

I start to put my shirt back on and then ask him again, because I can. Because I'm paying the tab and because I don't really like him. I want to annoy him. So I ask him again.

"You're sure?"

He sighs and decides to do me a favor and pull himself away from his phone, a phone that's probably running the damn app that I built. The same app that put me, Jeffery Sorbenstien, on the cover of fucking *Time* magazine last year. Me, the 29 year old man of the year. Me, THE motherfucking MAN of THE year. But instead of looking at me he moves on to flipping through the various forms and reports he has on one of those big folding metal tablets that doctors always use.

I made an app for that as well but with the all the new healthcare regulations coming into effect, I haven't been able to get the damn thing through beta testing. It has something to do with encryption, patient privacy, or some other such non-issue.

"I'm absolutely sure. Now if you'd like we can go over the results or we can go over what my team and I think would be the best treatment for this type of cancer," he says.

I'm gonna cut him off in a second. I already know exactly what it is that I am going to do and it doesn't exactly involve his form of treatment. I just want to get my other shirt on.

"Now we feel that it would be best to start out on an aggressive—"

"Nope, fuck that," I say looking him right in the eye again and interrupting him. He doesn't move.

"I'm sorry, Mr. Sorbenstein, did you say no?"

Now, this is the part where he's going to pay attention.

"You're damn right I said no. I'm the one footing the bill, aren't I? So I can say pretty much say whatever I want to say, at any point in time that I want to say it. And I am saying no. But don't worry, I am gonna tell you what it is that I am gonna do."

He stops thumbing through reports and looks at me. See, I told you he was going to pay attention.

"And what is that, Mr. Sorbenstien?"

I wait and stare for a few heartbeats right at him, right through him, long enough for him to get uncomfortable. Then I say it, the plan that I worked up right after I found out that I had cancer. Because I already knew the original results were correct. I just needed to be absolutely, one hundred percent sure. Plus, money isn't an issue for me, especially when you find out that you have cancer.

"I'm gonna freeze myself," I say.

"I'm sorry; did you just say that you were going to freeze yourself?" he asks me as if I've just spoken to him in some other language, and by the look on his face, it appears I am speaking something more akin to Aramaic than English.

"I sure did," I say, but our roles have become reversed.

Now I'm the one thumbing through my tablet, not giving him the time of day. I don't carry a phone. Talking, as the kids would say, is so last decade that it's tragic. Besides, everything that I do is on a tablet; I have no need for your puny phones, savages.

"Well, if you don't mind me saying, Jeff, that's insane. I mean, I know I just told you that you're dying of cancer and all but..."

I have things to do so I tune out my doctor-turned-father figure and work with the tablet, allowing my hands to do the talking, gathering intelligence, getting the business ends of things done. Potentially I will also divorce my wife today, so I want to get everything ready on that end as well.

I let him finish and there's an abnormally long pause as I auto correct the spelling in the email that I'm shooting to my lawyer. The doctor is waiting for a reply but I just hop down off the table in the examining room and move to leave. He'll get the email that he and his team are fired in a minute or so, maybe less. This is 5G shit I've got in my hands, I built out the whole network from scratch. It's not even been released to the public yet. It could be less than half of a half a minute.

"Did you just send me an email?" asks the man that just realized he's no longer on my personal payroll anymore.

"Yep, it's got some details in it about the press conference that I'm about to hold," I say without looking at him.

"Am I supposed to be there?" he asks in a frustrated tone that brings little buds of joy blooming in my ears.

"It's going to be right outside the hospital's front doors so if you want to show up then you can. If not, I don't give a shit. Your services are no longer needed."

I open the door to the reception area and walk out. When you're rich, you can get a private doctor. When you're rich and famous, say as famous as being "The Man of the Year," then you *need* a private doctor. I throw a brief smile and casual wave to the receptionist sitting behind the sliding glass window. My now former doctor walks out the *faux* woodgrain and metal doors a few seconds behind me.

"What should I tell the media?" he asks me again. Really, for someone who probably spent, conservatively, over a quarter million dollars on a degree you would think that the doc would be able to simply read his fucking emails.

"Tell them whatever you want to. You're no longer bound by any sort of Doctor-Patient privilege; I gave you those rights back in the email I just sent you," I say back to him, still moving towards his office front doors. My security team will be waiting just outside with more than a few 2.0 journalists and traditional media news readers.

I grab my jacket from the coat rack and pull it on, put the tablet into one of my pockets and get ready to open the door. I've had some time to think about what it is that I want to say, about thirty-five years, at least. I figure full disclosure about the freezing should be in order, let everyone know that I'm not going down without a fight, *et cetera*, *et cetera*. Also, knowing you're dying affords you a wider perspective on things: personal issues, public matters, business decisions and the like. I take in a deep breath before I put the big, shit-eating, five thousand dollar smile on my face.

The doctor stands there in his white coat and I can feel him staring like an asshole at the middle of my back, waiting for me to tell him I'm joking and that we can discuss the results later. I'm not joking; I'm tired. I hear the buzz starting outside the doors to his office.

I just informed the world through the tips of my fingers that there is going to be a press conference. I just became the hottest news story of the decade, yet again. I grab the polished nickel handle, turn it and fling the doors open to face the world.

There are already well over a dozen assorted bloggers, reporters and other journalists foaming at the mouth beyond my security detail, popping pictures, feeding live video streams, fingers blazing over their own tablets and even one guy with a laptop, archaic as that is. I wave. I smile. My security guys push back the thrum of electronics and questions, and we move past them towards the elevator. Someone asks where the press conference will be.

"Outside, in about five minutes or so," I say back without looking at whoever it was that asked.

The stainless steel on the elevator door is crisp and polished as a mirror; I take a quick look around in the reflection. The hallway is blindingly white, the plants are probably artificial, and the tiles on the floor look too clean for their own good. The art on the wall is too contemporary and my eyes look too deeply set in my head. The initial tests said I had a year, maybe less.

I am Mearsult in *The Stranger*, greeting the crowd, awaiting my death. It's the best I've felt in years.

* * *

The air outside is sharp and cool, it's springtime in Cleveland, which means that it's either going to be ridiculously hot soon or that it might snow. Northeast Ohio is tragically unpredictable when it comes to weather patterns.

My guess is that it has something to do with the fact that northeast Ohio is also the armpit of the world, too sticky or too dry, never just right.

I was born here. I went through a series of schools here. I went through a series of shitty jobs here. And I invented the most downloaded and heavily used app in the modern history of apps here. So when the big venture capitalists and investors came around, poking their noses into my app, my baby, I decided to stay. I single-handedly took this city from its stagnant forty-year-long hospice stay to thriving metropolis in less than three years. It wasn't LeBron James; it was Jeffrey Sorbenstein. The king is dead, long live the emperor.

New buildings are being built; startups and corporations are bringing new cash flows into the region, allowing businesses to actually come back down to the city center. It's so different from the way it used to be, back in the good old days, when you could walk around downtown and get mugged for the lint in your pocket and the cigarette in your hand.

It's clean now, sophisticated and scrubbed. I hate it. All of what made the city a hellish nightmare, a place you wanted to flee at all costs, a place that made you, through sheer force of will, want to do something better with your life, is now either muted or gone. It's the hottest place to live and the fastest growing city between New York and Chicago. We put the final nail in Detroit's coffin, which, to tell you the truth, felt pretty good because as much as I hate what Cleveland's become, I really, really, really hate Detroit.

The major news networks are trying to put up a podium full of microphones. The rest of the crowd is made up of everyday working journalists, pavement jockeys, muckrakers and students. All the regulars are here, and by regulars I mean Fox News, MSNBC, CNN, CSPAN, Prison Planet.com. But there's even more micro news outlets, community site bloggers, hyper local news feed burners, random freelancers and I'm sure some assortment of "others" that I'm totally missing.

THIS IS THE END

It's loud out on the street; there's an ambulance siren in the background, and the *thump thump thump* of a helicopter's beating wings drowns out everything for a few seconds as it lands on top of the hospital.

The crowd is making noise, talking about what the announcement could be. Each camp is trying to out scoop each other and under it all I hear the distinct current of electricity coming from all the devices everyone is carrying. Most likely they're all running some form of the app as well.

Across the street there is already a small assortment of protestors; the police have them cordoned off into a free speech cage. One of the cops is wrestling a third world country sort of thin girl to the ground and putting her jaw on a curb, another one is frisking an old lady for drugs. Welcome to the twenty-first century.

You would think that with the close proximity to "journalists," the cops wouldn't be this brazen, but then again, I'm news and they aren't. I'm rich, they're poor. The more things change, right?

My security guys are flanking me, scanning the crowd both here and across the street. They're waiting for the shots, or the grenades or anything else that might be immediately hazardous to my health. I keep telling them that it doesn't matter anymore, but they keep telling me, "As long as the checks keep coming, you'll die a very slow and painful death from cancer and nothing else."

The front of the clinic is pristine and modern, a glass obstruction to the marvels of the natural world. Seventy-five stories of pure architectural wonderment poking itself into the sky like a middle finger to God.

Someone from the back of the crowd wants me to get on with it already, someone else tells them to shut the fuck up or leave. I shake my head slightly and look down trying not to laugh.

This is the announcement of my eventual death, it should be somber; I should be more morose or melancholic, but I'm not. I don't care.

The audio visual tech signals that everything is ready to the lead man on my security team and he walks over to the podium and checks it again for whatever it is they check for, and then nods to me to come over.

I clear my throat. Everything goes quiet except the crowd across the street. I look at them and smile. I pull out a cigarette from my pack of American Spirits and light it. I take a long drag and I feel the cancer inside my chest grow. Every time I breathe it feels as if my lungs have gallons of chunky fluid in them.

"Good afternoon, everyone," I say into the vast conglomeration of microphones. There's a slight echo back.

"Thank you for joining me today on such short notice."

2.

After I make the initial announcement that I'm dying of cancer, and after I explain that it's not a joke—what else can I really say about it?—I wait for the eventual *"How are you going to treat it?"* question. It comes from a representative of MSNBC, state-run media if ever there was one in this country. Everyone thinks that Fox News is the GOP-run television network, which, of course, they are, but nobody ever questions where MSNBC gets all their funding from. Let me put that to rest: your tax dollars. I'm rich—I don't pay taxes.

"I've decided to freeze myself," I say, and a very literal hush falls over the crowd, even the protestors have shut up at this point.

Someone starts laughing. I don't know who it is exactly or else I would have called them out on it personally, so I look out at the crowd and smile.

"I'm sorry, I don't find any of this funny. This isn't a joke; I'm going to freeze myself until they find a cure." People stop laughing. Instantly fingers move across touchscreens. I can feel the zoom lenses coming in on my face like planes on King Kong, but I'm the emperor, I have the last laugh.

"You can't be serious?" asks one of the microbloggers, who I absolutely know for a fact wasn't shit until my app's advertising feature catapulted them into the big time.

"No, I'm *very* serious about all of this. I'm going to freeze myself until they find a cure, and then, when you're either all too old or all too dead to report on it, I'm going to wake up and live out the rest of my filthy rich life."

I look right into the microblogger's face and smile. I want him to know he may have a couple million, but I have nearly half a trillion in capital, liquid-fucking-capital, to do whatever I want with.

"What about your company?" asks one of the manicured plastic surgery beauties from Fox News.

"Look, everything will continue on. We have more than enough money to continue to destroy your brains with our apps for years to come," I say. People chuckle.

Then I start hitting them with big fucking atom bombs of truth. This was the plan all along. Okay, not all along, but at least since I found out I have cancer. I let the cigarette drop and grind it into the composite concrete steps that run under the small platform the podium is set up on.

"In fact, we're working with both the DHS and NSA on a project right now that will totally compromise the intelligence of generations to come."

I smile again and then let my face go serious. They smile back, but then start to get it. I'm not joking. I'm not having a laugh with them; I'm laughing at them.

"Are you being serious?" asks someone else from the megacorporations. I look right over to the Prison Planet.com guys.

"Yes, Alex Jones and his staff had it mostly right. I couldn't be more serious. Though, to tell you the truth, Alex works for the CIA as well. I mean, hasn't anyone wondered why he's still on the air if he's exposing real secrets?"

The crowd across the street goes wild with venomous joy, some of them even applaud. The journalists representing Prison Planet.com aren't having fun anymore.

Everyone else begins to yell. It's a feeding frenzy of questions. My security guys become restless. A cop puts another frail-looking student, this one appears to be a man or boy or whatever, that was attempting to reach our side of the road into the pavement.

"He was right about my corporation working with the two agencies; he was half-right about the facial recognition and biometric scanning software that allows you to tag your 'friends,' and almost right about my whole company being propped up by the government."

Fingers are moving at speeds that are probably not supposed to be possible for jointed appendages. Someone yells my name and I look over and point.

THIS IS THE END

"Why should we believe any of this?" they ask.

I let that one sit for a minute. And then, when I'm ready, I smile and flash the five thousand buck beauties at them and say, "Because…I'm fucking dying."

* * *

The news conference lasts another hour and fifteen minutes. It's physically exhausting, but I let it all out. I answer questions about why I'm freezing myself: "Because I can."

Why am I coming out now about everything? "Why the fuck not; what are they going to do to me? I'm already dying."

What do they think caused it? I hold up the next cigarette in my seemingly never-ending supply and then say, "Next."

Finally, after all the stupid questions, the silly, unimportant issues like what about my investors—"I bought them out and will be the sole owner of the company, even in suspended animation"—someone asks about my wife.

I look out into the faces of the crowd and say, "I haven't figured that one out yet, but I'm pretty sure I'm going to either kill her or divorce her."

The protestors across the street have all been let out of the free speech zone; the crowd has nearly tripled. Even the cops have slack jaws and are listening to me go on and on about the truth. The way the world really works. The way business is run: the back room deals, the underhanded way that everything is pushing us towards a total takeover of our lives by megacorporations, about how individuality is a lie, how being unique is really a way to market products to sub-niche groups. The revolution wasn't televised, it was advertised, branded, bought and sold, to you, for you, by you. And you just eat it up.

After I've said my piece, after I answer the last few questions, I've had enough of their glass-eyed looks and yapping maws to end it, plus I have things to do and money to spend before I freeze myself.

So I wave, shoot the bird out to everyone and say, "Thanks, folks. Fuck you."

I turn to leave. My security guards make a tight circle around me. Big dudes who have more technology, testosterone and weaponry than should legally be allowed fold in around me like a wall of meat and we move back into the lobby of the hospital. The sun is low in sky and my chariot awaits; I'm flying out to my office on a private helicopter.

We make our way into the elevator and up to the landing pad on top of the hospital that's normally reserved for life flight choppers. My black bird is there waiting for me. The blades are spinning enough for me to bend over slightly. As we pull away I look down at the front of the hospital. The crowd is still there, standing like those Terracotta Warriors in China, silent and fragile, endless and broken.

3.

I check my email on the tablet while the chopper makes its decent towards the roof of my building. I want to see what the world is saying about my little truth sit-in. All the usual suspects have spun it to make it sound as if I've lost my fucking mind. The market has dipped a bit, especially in the tech sector, but the underlying news that I have more apps coming out has hedged any sort of short sells that might have happened due to my chat with the public. Alex Jones is adamantly denying that he works for the CIA. I look away and down towards the landing pad.

I see two figures standing on top of the roof. One of whom is my lawyer, who I am happy to see—go figure. The other is my soon-to-be ex-wife, who I am obviously not so happy to see.

By now the video of the press conference has had enough time to go around the world three or four thousand times, but I knew this moment was coming. I'm not going to lie to you though; I was sort of hoping that I wouldn't have to deal with it until right before I freeze myself. It's a character trait I've always had, and it goes like this: as much as I like to make a shit, I don't actually like having to deal with the smell of it.

I need a cup of coffee and another cigarette. I also *need* to finalize a couple of things that shouldn't take me more than a day or so. But seeing her standing there on the landing pad—her hair cut and colored the wrong way for her ugly, frown-lined face but the right way for whatever passes as fashionable—tells me that this is going to seriously suck big balls.

I recognize the fact that announcing my intent to get a divorce publicly is a shitty thing to do. I get it, I know, blah-blah-blah. But in the spirit of being honest, I did only marry her for her dad's money. Yes, I am a terrible person, one who probably deserves cancer. However she has never had to work in her life, never had to make decisions and sacrifices, never wanted for anything. Ever. So I think the half-billion dollar payout that's sitting in her bank account, right about now, is enough to completely compensate her for the emotional damages I may have caused. Believe me; she'll forgive me when she sees that. Also, I really fucking hate her.

I lean back in my seat a little and hold my breath as we set down on the roof. The most dangerous times during a flight are at takeoffs and landings, and helicopters are pretty fucking scary things to do both of those in. I tell the lead security guy—James, I think his name is; I don't really know because they rotate out so frequently, and also given the fact that I don't care—that he should wait for my signal to escort her out of the building.

He nods and whispers something into his watch that isn't really a watch, and the rest of the security guards nod in unison. I'm not sure, but I think we built those watches, too.

She's waiting, trying to hold her whatever-the-fuck haircut in place. My lawyer stands off a little further from the landing pad; he looks like a robot, still and unwavering. Not even a single hair is misplaced by the downdraft from the chopper as it lands. He has a tablet like mine, they are both synched to each other and I update him with real time. Not fake real time, mind you, not three-, or five-, or even half-second delayed "real time." I mean as-I-see-the-world-through-my-eyes, nanosecond real time. Let me put it to you this way: by the time I've typed it, he's already read it. It usually makes dealing with issues such as this much easier.

As the rotors die down I can almost hear her screaming at me and telling me to get out. The windows are completely blacked out so that you can't see in, but she's flown in the chopper before and knows exactly where I sit, exactly where to look me in the eye. I sigh and pull out my pack of smokes, check my count and realize that I have to grab another pack before I head out again. My hand moves towards the latch on the door, and I pull it down and then slide it open.

She starts, "You're divorcing me?"

"No, I just said that because I thought it would be a lark, a laugh, something to do," I sigh and then add, "Yes," without looking at her. I've never threatened to hit anyone before, especially a woman, but if I look at her right now, I might have to break that streak.

"Jesus Christ, Jeff, you just announced that you were going to divorce me at a press conference. What the hell were you thinking?"

I continue to walk past her. I don't have to look at her; our contract has been fulfilled and we're through. I pull out the tablet and continue to walk towards my lawyer. She insists on following me. I look over at my lead security guy. He does the curt sort of nod thing and then motions for two of his men to take her by both arms.

"What are you doing, Jeff?" she asks. Then she realizes what's going on and begins to yell at the silverbacks in suits that follow me around. "Get your goddamn hands off me! Do you throwbacks even know who I am?"

Neither of the two men says a word. They continue to usher her past me and my lawyer, towards the door.

She starts kicking and screaming at me. "Fuck you, Jeff. I *want* a divorce so I can take this stupid company, that app and everything you own away from you." She says all of this and more as the shaved apes parade her through the access door and into the stairwell.

I wait until after she's gone and then look up at my lawyer, Phil Goldstein, the only man I trust more than myself.

Again, go figure.

He's still standing like a statue; every bit of him is composed. There's not a single speck of dust, dirt, hair or residue from the rooftop on his black suit. His chin looks chiseled out of stone; his hair is cropped and pulled back into a tight and conservative pencil-straight side part. Seriously, if I didn't know better I would have my doubts that he was human.

"Phil, how are you?" I ask as we begin to walk towards the door. The sun is setting and there's a chill running through the wind.

I want to get a hot cup of coffee and I still have some business to attend to, final drafts and some minor coding to get to tonight.

"Good, Jeff. I just finished depositing the settlement into Janet's account, notified her lawyers and they have agreed to accept the terms of the divorce," he says back as we move through the door and down a flight of steps that leads towards my office.

My security detail moves in front of us through the door. Many of them are going home; the second shift will be clocking in and waiting for me outside my office when we get there. I don't really like the security. I only keep them around because I feel bad that they'll soon be out of work.

I won't need the entire detail when I'm frozen, maybe just one or two a day and one or two of them at night. So I figure that I can, at the very least, give them all the overtime they want until I go to sleep.

Phil walks me through the door that leads to the hallway that leads to the only place I really feel at home, my office. God, I love my office. I will probably miss my office more than I miss anything else after I've been frozen. Okay, maybe not cigarettes, but it'll be a very close second. I have even left explicit instructions that there's to be absolutely no major changes in the layout of my office—just minor upgrades, mostly tech-based—while I'm asleep.

I bought this building with the first hundred million I made, gutted it and had the top floor of the old factory and manufacturing space turned into my own private office. There's close to 12,000 square feet of space in it. I love it; it's tacky and ultra-modern and cold and devoid of any real color. It's clean and simple, mine and mine alone. I have a secretary, but she's just here from the traditional nine-to-five. I basically live here. There's a fully functioning bathroom and kitchen, two loft bedrooms that you could conservatively fit three king-sized beds in and still have enough room to hold a dinner party for twelve, and, of course, spiral staircases—two huge, ugly, wrought iron spiral staircases that I rescued from a building that they were ripping down across town.

The doors are completely bulletproof—not resistant, but bulletproof. The windows are floor-to-ceiling length and covered with a new solar membrane that helps power the array of computers, personal servers and appliances that are in the space. We manufacture the polymers and membranes, as well. They don't make as much money as the apps do, but I get healthy research and development grants from the Pentagon for the designs so I really can't complain.

The doors to my office run biometric finger scan security protocols, so Phil and I stop discussing the weather long enough for me to scan in and get inside. After I hear the magnetic click of the locks, I stop in the doorway and take stock of the simplistic, awesome beauty. I take in the smell of coffee and old cigarettes and the thin white noise of electronics as they hum hundreds of thousands of processes per second.

Okay, I admit it, I'm gonna miss my office more than my smokes. There's a huge semi-circular desk that sits in the middle of the "official" business section of the space and I move to sit in the perfectly sized and expertly molded, ergonomically designed specifically for me executive chair sitting in the middle of the opening.

I touch the screens that are mounted into the desk and my coffee maker in the kitchen begins to brew a fresh pot of coffee. I ask Phil if he wants a cup and he shakes his head no.

"Down to business, then?" I ask him. He begins tapping his tablet and I watch as the other screens mounted around the desk console come to life and start scrolling pictures of the nearly completed cryogenic chamber that I'm going to be freezing myself in. I watch as men in white, freeze-dried space suits assemble the last few pieces.

Tubes jut at angry angles from every side; there are huge tanks that I presume hold the stuff that they are going to use to freeze my body strapped to the wall next to the large glass coffin-like structure where my actual physical body will be placed. I won't be in there just rotting from the inside either; I'll be under going chemotherapy in there as well as some of the latest organic and chemical treatments that my money can buy. There's also a failsafe, a just-in-case, built in to the life support systems. I mean, you can't be too careful when you're undergoing one of the first long-term freezes of the twenty-first century.

ERIC POLLARINE

I hear the coffee as it finishes brewing and move to get a cup. It's one of the last cups of coffee I'll have in a long, long time. It's delicious.

4.

Phil and I discuss the status of my "Freeze chamber." I opted for that description being used as "Cryotank" sounds a bit too Goth for my tastes, but really you could call it a high-tech meat freezer for all I care. As long as it works the way it's supposed to and I come out alive in the end, I don't give a shit. We talk about the company's holdings, the future, the apps and developments that I want the company to focus on, and a couple of last minute changes to my "Living will"—all digital and pre-recorded versions.

Then we move to some of the black ops, skunkworks stuff that we've been working on: hybrid stealth holographic projection membranes for tanks and planes, railgun technology for the Navy and, of course, a couple of chemical and neurological weapons. I don't like the way I have to do business, but you're fooling yourself if you think that you can take money from the government and not owe them something for it.

I told most of the truth today at the press conference, or at least the amount of truth that I can really tell when it comes to the company's involvement with the government. But I've also come to realize, all intended Star Wars references aside, that the truth, the real truth, really just means "a certain point of view."

Phil continues to try and explain how we're developing a crowd control aerosol dispersant with some name that I can't pronounce even if I have it phonetically spelled out for me. I'm really good at computers—coding and scripting languages, data management, HTML and CSS 6—meaningless, fake and intrinsically ethereal things like that. Hardcore scientific shit like this on the other hand, has and will always be a mystery to me.

It's nearly midnight after we call the day officially done. I've almost finished off a second pot of coffee and Phil looks less like a statue and more like the tired and graying high-powered lawyer that he is. I smile at him and tell him to call it an early night.

He gets up and we shake hands. I put my finger on the console and the magnetic locks click open, allowing the doors to swivel open slightly. The second shift security guys glance into the room and then hold open the big, heavy doors for Phil as he exits. They release and the doors automatically close. I've got a few things to do before I can get to bed, but I pass out at the desk somewhere around one thirty, maybe later.

* * *

When I used to dream, I used to have the same dream over and over again, almost every night. I say almost because, on the nights that I wouldn't have the same dream, I wouldn't dream at all. But more to the point, I've been having the same dream for nearly thirty years, which I'm sure that if I could find a psychologist—or is it a psychiatrist? Or whichever of the two that would be most qualified to interpret dreams—if I could find one of those people who could explain what it meant, then I'm sure it wouldn't be a very positive or healthy explanation.

The dream goes like this: *I'm standing on top of the tallest structure in the world. I'm standing there naked, holding my arms out and letting the wind have its way with me, pushing me back and forth, swaying over the edge. Below the building there are thousands of people, maybe millions staring up at me, eying me, making me feel as if I'm the center of the universe. They look as if they're praying to me or to the heavens or to something else completely different. I was never a very religious guy so I couldn't tell you, but they're praying to something. And I couldn't care less, I'm just there, arms outstretched and I feel the heat of the sun on my body.*

I finally lose my balance and fall. But it's a graceful fall; it's like a great, big elegant swan dive into the sea of people, giant people now, as everything comes rushing up, distorted and off perspective. I crash into them and blood and bone and fragments of their bodies collide with my own and I'm drowning in them. But I don't care—I'm smiling. I'm at peace with myself, with this outcome, the falling, the nakedness, at peace with everything.

I know; it's completely fucked up.

THIS IS THE END

* * *

I wake up in a small puddle of foul-smelling drool. Ah, the glamorous life of a multi-billion dollar internet mogul; there's no huffing handfuls of cocaine off of high-priced hooker ass for me. Nope, just stagnant morning breath mixed with the acid from last night's coffee and a weird metallic taste in my mouth that I attribute to the desktop. My neck feels like it's been in a vice all night and I move my hand over the screen to see what time it is. My stomach growls and I begin to freak out when I see that it's nearly noon.

Carol, my secretary, should be at her desk outside the main office by now. I call out and ask her to patch me through to the kitchen in the cafeteria downstairs.

I order breakfast and then get up to make some more coffee. But I'm really late in getting some very important things accomplished, so I skip all the formalities and microwave whatever coffee was left over from the night before. I'm going to see my father today.

Carol wheels in the breakfast shortly after I get out of the shower. I'm still soaking wet when I come down out of the bathroom. She's used to me being less than discreet in front of her. I mean, it's not like I'm naked or anything, but it's not like I'm modest, either. And I know what you're thinking and let me say that, *no*, I never cheated on my now ex-wife with Carol.

Though, now that she's my ex-wife, I might have sex with Carol just because. I think about it for a few seconds and then realize I probably won't have time to suggest anything like that. I'm being frozen in less than 48 hours. Besides, I can bang one out tonight by myself if I really need to.

I eat in what feels like seconds, inhaling the French toast and hash browns. I move back to getting ready. Along with my leftover coffee and breakfast, I have to take a rather substantial regimen of vitamins and pills that will help in the freezing process. After dinner tonight I won't be able to eat anything solid ever again. I need to have a completely free digestive tract for the freezing process; you can imagine what it would be like if you were frozen with a stomach full of heavy foods for who knows how long. I've also been assured that it would not be a pretty picture when or if I thaw out.

I skip shaving, combing my hair and anything else other than putting on clothing to expedite the process. Halfway through pulling on my undershirt I start in on a coughing fit. I've been having these since before I found out that I had cancer. In fact, the coughing is left over from a nasty chest cold that I had about six months ago and is actually what sparked my regular doctor to test for cancer.

Chunks of lung come gurgling up the back of my throat and I spit out a thick, semi-greenish-black paste into the toilet. I check the toilet to find that there's now little flecks of rust on the hunks coming out.

"That's new," I say into the toilet bowl. As I'm flushing I hear the sounds of footsteps in my office.

"Jesus, Carol, I told you: I have important things to do today," I say as I move back towards the main part of my office. I take a few steps towards the figures then stop in my tracks as the outline of his face comes into focus and swallow hard.

"Hello, Jeff," says the head of the Department of Homeland Security. I instantly regret holding my little press conference yesterday. There are some people that even money cannot impress or buy. The head of The Department of Homeland Security is one of them. I've tried.

5.

"Robert, what a pleasant surprise," I manage to say without sounding like I've just made the front of my pants dark. I look over at the two very, very large pieces of genetically modified gorilla meat in suits—most likely carrying large amounts of weaponry—that are flanking Robert McMillan, Head and Secretary of The Department of Homeland Security; an entity, until recently, that we had been working with developing all sorts of…well, you got the details at the press conference.

He moves like a man shouldn't. Like a shadow on the wall. Like something that doesn't quite exist in this sphere of reality: silent, hulking and powerful. He moves towards one of the floor-to-ceiling windows and rests his hand on it. He looks back and starts to make polite conversation.

"Looks like you've made a lot of progress with these solar membranes," he begins to ramble, but I cut him off midway through.

"Look, Rob," I try to emphasize the fact that I can call him Rob and that I know he hates it. "I really don't have time for this, so if you're going to kill me then get it over with, but please just have one of your Neanderthals shoot me in the fucking head. I don't want to sit here and be bored to death by formalities."

He looks back out the widow, still seemingly enthralled by the progress on the solar membranes, not even bothering to acknowledge he's in my office, in my building, in my city.

"You know what your problem is, Jeff?" he asks. Though I know where this is all leading, I humor him as I finish putting on the rest of my clothes.

"Um, the three of you standing in my office, breathing my nice colloidal silver-purified air?" I say back to him as I finish buttoning up my overshirt. I'm visiting my father today so I figured that I would get dressed up. Give the old man one last middle finger before I go completely rigid.

"You've always been barely tolerable, Jeff. Now that you're dying, you're even less than that," he says before turning back to look at me with the two evil, grey, soul sucking voids he calls eyes. We kind of have a history.

I reach for my coat, which I had thrown over one of the chairs in the little seating area that is stationed just off the side of the main room from my desk command center. I barely have time to finish pulling on my left sleeve when I feel his hand come across my throat and grip down. For a man in his fifties, he's incredibly fast—probably some form of enhancement that we made for the Department which he injected into himself. I feel the air rush out of my throat and my lungs begin to fill with fire and pain from lack of breathable oxygen.

"You little shit," he snarls into my ear as he pulls my face closer to his.

"You wrecked Project Mobile yesterday with your little fucking truth hiccup. Do you know how hard it's been on the Department's PR staff to try and cover up what you leaked? Do you?"

I can't do anything except look like a sissy pulling at the augmented strength in the vise-grips he calls a hand around my throat. I don't even try to breathe. Just keep it cool, keep me alive.

"Do you even remember who lent you your first hundred million? It was my agency; we made your little power trip possible." His eyes are mad, fireballs of anger. He's squeezing harder and harder, my eyes bulge out and I try to look around the room but all I see are wisps of purple and streaks of silver fireworks.

"I should do the world a favor and just end your piece of shit life here and now." He releases the claw from around my throat and I slump to the floor, taking one of the chairs with me, toppling it over on its side. I begin to suck in great gasps of air, my chest and heart and head all throb like one large, swollen organ. He looks down at me and smiles, fixing his stupid, ugly, cheap tie.

"But I'm not. I'm going to let your spoiled ass do whatever it is that you want to do because after tomorrow, you'll be frozen. And what more can you really do then?"

"Ever the compassionate conservative, huh, Rob? How's that third presidential bid going for you?" I ask trying to massage the words from out of my neck, and then it hits me.

I look up over at him and he knows I just got it, too. His mouth is a crooked jack-o'-lantern grin.

"How did you know it was tomorrow?" I ask him, though I already know the answer, so it was more of a rhetorically stunned, stupid thing to say. I try to push myself back up using the overturned chair, and then I decide that maybe the room shouldn't spin and that I should remain on the floor.

"Don't play stupid, Jeff. I know you're not," he says walking towards my door. The two things that parade as human beings flank him.

"Just know that you'll be frozen, and I won't be. Good luck, son, and say high to your father for me," he says. Then I hear him knock on the door. It swings open a second or two later, and I see that my own security detail is seated, along with Carol, on the couch out in the main waiting room.

There are two more thugs pointing big, black plastic-looking guns at their faces. Carol gives me a look to say she's sorry. I nod back to her and explain that I get it.

I wait a few more minutes on the floor and then I need a cigarette, so I slide back up the chair. The room doesn't do the whole merry-go-round thing and I walk towards my desk and grab my pack. I wave my hand over the screens and start typing out code.

6.

I look at the hieroglyphic strings of code covering the screens and make sure to save it three times: once to the onsite servers, once to all three of the five-terabyte portable hard drives that are strapped under the desk, and once to the offsite backup server centers. My throat has neat little bruises in the shape of Robert's fingers and thumb on it and I'm finally able to swallow without making a sickening cracking sound. I look at the time, it's nearly four and I still have to see my father. I run a quick check on the code again and then minimize the editor on the screen and wave my hands to send them to sleep. I can finalize this little last "fuck you" later. I have things to do.

I call out to see if Carol and the security detail are still here. One of the meat puppets answers, "*Yes, sir. What can we do for you?*"

I hesitate for a few seconds before asking the nameless voice to have someone bring my car around so I can visit my father. I'm going to do this myself. No large security details, no lawyers; I want this to be a private viewing only. It's the last time I am going to see him ever, so I want it to be memorable, without the benefit of having hairless apes standing around whispering to each other about their quadrant being "all clear" and if they've seen the latest this or that. I make sure he understands and to tell everyone that I won't be gone for longer than an hour or so and that in the event that I don't come back, not to worry. Checks are going to be deposited anyway.

"*Very good, sir. I'll have someone bring around your car; ETA on that will be fifteen minutes.*"

I say, "Thanks," and click off the phone, wave my hand in front of my screens again, and type a few commands that bring up video feeds of the white-suited scientists putting the finishing touches on the freeze chamber.

No matter how certain you are about something, a plan of action, decision, or what have you, there's always room for doubt. Like when I started building my app. I knew, in the back of my mind, that it would do everything it needed to do. I knew that it was my ticket off the whole shitty job after shitty job ride. I knew that marrying Janet was the wrong decision but that it would be a larger gain in the long run. I knew that staying in Cleveland would change it for the better.

But even in all of those decisions there were moments of doubt like the one I'm having right now. Nagging suspicions, the sickening realization that you could be wrong, that all of these choices were going to backfire. Janet's dad could have said no, the app could have been a failure, staying in Cleveland could have killed my company's future. As I watch the last diagnostic tests being run, I know full well that this could wind up being a huge waste of time and money.

The cancer could go on eating at the inside of my body, hollowing me out, leaving a sunken husk. Or I could simply not survive the freezing process.

But, given the situation, dying wouldn't be all that bad. I would just be dead. At least I wouldn't have to deal with cancer, or quarterly earning reports, or Janet popping up in every tabloid imaginable hanging on the arm of whatever flavor of the month she would inevitably be banging to try and get back at me for divorcing her.

I said I was never unfaithful, I never said that she wasn't. But all of that doesn't matter if you're dead. And technically speaking, even if the freezing process doesn't kill me, I'm already on my way to being dead. My phone cracks to life snapping my head back to look at it like it was something foreign. The voice on the other side says, "*Mr. Sorbenstein, your car is ready in the garage. Do you need an escort down?*"

I shake my head as if he can see me, and then say, "No." I get up and grab my jacket and then head to the bar to grab a bottle of something really expensive. It's time to see dear old dad.

I open the doors and the security guards that looked so impotent sitting on the couch with Carol have gotten back some of their dignity and stand up to walk me to the elevator doors. I turn around and tell them to get something to eat—whatever they want from the cafeteria, on me—and push the door closed button and head down to the parking deck below the building.

It takes all of three seconds until the saccharine-sweet female computerized voice says, "*Garage. Thank you,*" and I exit and stare at my beautiful car.

For someone with enough money to buy a whole country's debt off, when I do drive, I try to drive as inconspicuous a car as possible.

I have a 2003 Ford Focus, which I know sounds ridiculous for one of the world's richest men to be driving a Ford Focus, but then again, you've never driven my Ford Focus. I had the body reinforced and bulletproof glass installed. I swapped out the shitty four-cylinder and upgraded it to a zippy little dual-eight. The wheels are all steel reinforced, 500 mile run-flats. I have enough cans of fix-a-flat to get me another 500 miles in the hatchback. The interior controls have all been upgraded as well.

The thing is literally a rolling version of my office: motion sensing heads-up displays with picture-in-picture capable touch sensitivity, connected 5G support, more of the solar membranes that I manufacture are installed over the rear and side windows, carbon fiber and Kevlar grey paint. And a nice little seven-shot 40 mm Glock tucked away in the glove compartment, just in case. Seriously, if I had a cannon installed it would be a fucking tank and, yes, I have thought about having a cannon installed.

I get in and push the ignition button and the little metal and technology-filled rhino purrs to life. I sync my tablet up to the GPS and throw it in drive leaving the city lights, the staggering drunks in the warehouse district along with the leftover remnants of homeless people, the Terminal Tower, Public Square and the rest of the godforsaken city behind in my rearview mirror.

* * *

The drive out to see my dad is a pretty long affair; he's in a far-lying suburb. It's technically not part of Cuyahoga County but it's also close enough that you could call it a suburb of Cleveland. Especially since Cleveland has begun to spread its wings further and further out, assimilating the immediate and even some of the furthest-lying suburbs. Like I said before, everyone wants to be here now. Even Ohio State has a huge new satellite campus here. It's nearly as big as the actual one in Columbus, and there's been talk that the school might have to split itself into two main branches in the very near future.

I went to Cuyahoga Community College but dropped out right after I started making history books and magazine covers. Eventually they decided to give me an honorary associate's degree in computer science. Not that I went there for it, nor did I have any interest in computer science when I was there, but it was still nice enough of them to hand me the shiny piece of scrap paper. It also doesn't hurt to donate enough money for the college to build a brand new building. After that, well, you can pretty much guarantee that I was going to get something other than a tax write-off for the gesture.

I pull through the gates and the security guard smiles and waves at me. I arranged for this ahead of time and I'm the only one here right now. I made sure that they not let anyone else in until I'm gone. I also donated enough money to have a new front gate built here, as well.

I don't come out to see my dad all that often, and it's kind of weird when I do. I visit my mom nearly every week, but I guess me and the old man have some unfinished business or something. Though, really, I just fucking hate him.

I park the car and walk up the grassy incline to where he's at. On the way I pull out the bottle of Laphroaig 1998 ten-year from my jacket. It's not the top of my collection, and my dad was more of a Dewar's White Label kind of guy, but fuck him for not having money or taste. This is about what I like. And also shoving the fact that I can afford to have taste down his throat will, at the very least, make me feel better.

I pass by the flat black pieces of granite and marble shining in the late day sun. It's another perfect day. The sky is motionless and clear. The wind is brisk but mellow. Nothing like it should be right now, raining and grey, the way it should always be in a cemetery. I walk further in to the sprawling park; I pass by little dogwoods, larger magnolias and some maples that are just about done unfurling their leaves, then I finally find the large flat opening that his plot is in.

I stare at the open grass; every plot around him has a stone, every stone has a name. It's a pretty standard and scenic cemetery: lots and trees, some larger stones, well-manicured grass and a lake with a shrine to some forgotten Saint Whoever. I look back down to the empty piece of land without a marker and I smile. Once I'm frozen, or gone, or whatever, no one will ever know he's here. It's my way of saying no one ever needed you. My way of saying that no one needs to know you ever lived, ever fathered children, ever held down a miserable job. No one needs to ever know you divorced three women and hurt anyone and everyone you ever knew. You're nothing now. You're just an open piece of land covered in goose shit. A plot of dirt that, in a hundred years, if anyone is still burying people in the fucking ground, they will dig up and put someone else on top of. Maybe it'll be someone who will deserve a stone, someone who'll deserve something to remember them by.

I crack open the bottle of whisky and the sweet, peaty smell makes me feel calm. I look down at the grass and sigh. I look out towards the lake, towards the water as its surface breaks black and gold. Tiny waves from the handful of ducks swimming in it lap at the pea stone shores that edge around it. I take a swig off the bottle. I know a whisky like this deserves a nice rock glass, maybe something in cut crystal, but right now I'm just visiting and I forgot to bring a glass.

The whisky burns my throat and chest for a few seconds. I feel like I'm going to start coughing again but then the fiery peat grain dissolves into a warm, slow campfire and I can breathe clearly. I'm pretty sure the cure for cancer is whisky. I light up a cigarette and then regret it, because I start coughing. I take another pull off the bottle; this one is slower and I stare down at the grass.

"I remember you though," I say. "Every goddamn day that comes around on this stupid Earth, every time I look in a mirror, I remember you."

I pull the bottle back towards my mouth again but stop and move to my cigarette instead. I turn the bottle upside down and let it pour over the grass and goose shit. The ground is still cold, so as the warm whisky hits, it makes little ghost vapors. I let the whole bottle drain out and then let the empty drop on the plot. I suck back on the cigarette and say, "Goodbye."

I walk back to my little Ford, get in and drive. The security guard at the gate raises his hand to wave at me and I don't look over at him. I'm crying. I will never come back to see my father ever again. I'm all right with that.

7.

The drive back into the city is far less picturesque than the drive out. Maybe it's the doubts about tomorrow, or maybe it's the fact I just spent the better part of my day either being nearly choked to death or crying like a little girl over a dead man that I hate, but I feel nauseous when I start seeing the concrete and urban sprawl begin to overtake the calm greenery of the suburbs. The sun is a burning, red eye, making the sunset, the last sunset I'll see for a while, as brilliant as it should be. Pink and purple streams of puffy cloud cover roll out towards the horizon line. I can't see Lake Erie from here but I'm sure that the view back in my office is pretty spectacular.

I hit a small pocket of traffic going back into the city and it gives me enough time to tap out a request for Phil to meet me at my office. Tomorrow is the big day and I want to make absolutely sure that there are no surprises in the form of DHS or any other three-letter department of the government. I pass by some well-dressed couples out for a little stroll down East 4th and then probably over to Playhouse Square to catch something by someone famous. I don't contribute to the arts as much as I probably should. I will tell Phil to do so tonight.

When I finally make it to the opening of the parking garage I'm greeted by more security guys. They flag me through and then close the steel roll down doors. They allow me the courtesy of getting out of my car by myself and then escort me back towards the elevator doors.

I light up another cigarette as I get into the polished chrome cylinder and push the button for my office. It takes another three seconds to get back up to the top.

"*Top floor. Thank you,*" says the horrible computer voice as I exit and I remind myself that I need to have that changed before I freeze. I feel like there's so much more to do, so much more that I should be doing. But tomorrow is the day and I'm not going to postpone this for anything. When I look up I see Phil sitting on the couch tapping something on his tablet. He stands up and moves towards me and we shake hands. It hits me that this is probably going to be the last time I shake Phil's hand. He gives me a weird look back as if I just said, "This is going to be the last time I shake your hand." He asks "What?"

I say, "It's nothing," and press my finger on the scanner. The doors click open and we move inside.

* * *

"Rob was here?" he says back to me, it's more a statement than a question, but I answer back with a head nod. He looks around and finds the chair that I was thrown into still on its side, then brings his hand to his forehead and starts rubbing. "Jesus."

"I know, and he said that there might be some problems tomorrow," I say as I move towards the kitchen to make a pot of coffee.

Phil looses his tie without looking up at me. "Let me guess, your little press conference."

"Yeah, he wasn't happy. He mentioned something about Project Mobile," I say back as I finish pouring the water into the reservoir and flick the on button.

"Also, I'm about to have my last meal; do you care to join me?" I ask.

He picks his head up from his hand and says, "Actually, I would be honored."

I sit back down in my chair and smile. "You're a terrible liar, Phil. I'm paying you well, and you're not honored."

I motion for the screens to come back to life and bring up the code I wrote earlier today. I know what "Project Mobile" is, but I decide to let Phil talk for a few as I'm deciding to on what I want for my last meal.

"Why don't you refresh my memory on that particular little outing?" I ask as I go back over the strands of code, checking to see if I used the right version of the languages, the right syntax and characters. I know I did, but I want the bug to work, so double-checking isn't a bad idea.

"What, you want me to tell you about Project Mobile? I thought we were having dinner."

"Humor me. Besides, you can have anything you want tonight, the best drinks, food and desert you'll probably ever eat. Also, I'm dying."

He laughs and looks around the office then says, "No, Jeff, you've already used up all your 'I'm dying' credits. You'll have to try something else."

"How about not paying you?" I say back to him stonefaced and serious enough that he decides not to call my bluff.

"It's your time and money," he shrugs and says back with a smile.

8.

I ordered stuffed steak with mashed potatoes, green beans, boiled carrots, fried apples, sweet potatoes and finished it all off with a small German chocolate cake for desert. Phil decided he would have something healthy and ordered a Kobe steak, salad with a pear vinaigrette dressing and some sort of onion soup thing. It smelled and looked like vomit.

While we eat he tells me about "Project Mobile," how we're developing ghost apps that will be running behind the two main operating systems all over the world, effectively turning all mobile devices everywhere into little beacons of streaming information. I look on unimpressed.

"How is that any different from what the government has been doing since 1996, when cell phones started becoming homing devices?"

He shakes his head.

"You're not seeing the big picture here, Jeff. It's not just beaming info out, it's beaming info in—straight to the user's eyes and ears. Subliminal signals, multiple digital frames and tones per second. Imagine being able to beam pro-Western messages into the heads of Chinese children 24 hours a day, seven days a week. Or Iranian children, soldiers, women. Hell, imagine being able to beam stand-down orders into the heads of every army on the face of the earth—except ours."

I can't believe what Phil is saying, but it makes sense now. All the work we've been doing, all the secrecy. I keep out of most of it. I know about pieces, but not the whole puzzle.

I know it now, though, and the code that I worked on today isn't going to help any. I look down at all the unfinished food; I suddenly no longer have an appetite.

"That's fucking brilliant," I whisper into my plate.

"I know," says Phil. I look up and he's looking out towards the city skyline. I join him. The distant blinking lights of communication towers look like earthbound stars; windows in office complexes form binary Rorschach tests. Stoplights and cars pass by in time with imaginary dance club rhythms. The real stars in heaven are eclipsed by LEDs and fluorescent bulbs powered by burning dinosaur bones. The world is small and silent.

I look back at him and he pulls himself away from the window, then smiles and says, "That was delicious." I nod and then move to the bar and open another bottle of Laphroaig—but this is just the regular ten-year—pour two dry glasses, then walk back and hand him one. I pull the pack of cigarettes out of my pocket and light one up. I begin to wonder what the fuck else we're doing for them that seems as crazy as this, but stop.

"Is there anything we can do?" I ask him, but I know there isn't. We signed over our souls a long, long time ago for funding.

He takes a sip of his whisky and shakes his head. "No, the project has gotten out of control. Do you want to know how much debt they're burning through just to get this done?"

I think about it for a few seconds and take a drag off the cigarette. It makes me want to cough, but then nicotine and whisky flood my internal sensors, calming my lungs down enough to avoid the spell.

"No, I guess in the long run it doesn't matter."

He holds his glass up in the air and leans back in his chair and toasts, "Here's to the brave new world."

"To the promise land," I say back and clink the air.

We go on to drink the whole bottle and half of another before the night is over.

9.

I wake up and immediately want to puke. I reach the kitchen in time to run the water in the sink and then I let loose a stream of projectile vomit that would make the effects people on the set of *The Exorcist* jealous. I try breathing, but start coughing as more bile and liquor fight their way up the back of my throat. I slump over the sink and try to aim, but really, right now, it's a crap shoot.

"Oh, sweet hell," I manage to gasp out before moving back towards the sink. I'm supposed to be getting frozen for years and years to come and the last thing I want is to be frozen with a fucking hangover. There's a man inside my head and he is beating a tympani to death with an elephant. I try to open my eyes and then quickly realize that the pulsing thump behind my eyeballs is enough to make me never want to see anything ever again. I close them quickly and try to make my way down towards the floor. I feel like I'm burning up on the inside. I make it halfway down the cabinet but then come slamming down to the ground. My hand is covered in vomit and I feel as if I'm going to shoot more of last night over everything for a third time.

My nose and eyes and mouth and throat all burn with the taste of liquor and acid. It smells worse than it actually tastes. I'm covered in it. I gently open my right eye and the room does a fantastic swirl. I lean over and lay my head down on the cool linoleum as gently as I possibly can. I begin to cry. But it's not tears of joy, or sadness, or pain, it's just precious water trying to escape the horrible feeling inside my body.

The floor soothes me back into a state of semi-consciousness. My brain starts to try and process what it is that I have to do today. The sober part of my brain, the one part of your brain that always makes you regret every shitty thing you've ever done in your entire life, starts to yell at me about timetables and procedures that I'm late for. I try to open one of my eyes again, but I couldn't tell you which one this time. It's closest to the floor; I think it's my left one. I see the melted orange juice concentrate pools of puke on the floor in front of me.

The light from the windows is bright but not sunny. I hear the pitter-patter of rain drops across the windows. They sound like tiny gunshots going off; everything is too loud. I know that I have to move; I know I have to try and get to the phone system and call for Carol or a doctor—anyone with anything to make this go away—but I can't. *Lying slumped over on the floor is a good plan*, says the rest of my brain, the part that's still trying to fight off the bottle and a half of whisky. I look over towards the cabinets; I catch my reflection in the stainless steel dishwasher. I look terrible, like a corpse, rotten and green. I feel it start somewhere in my abdomen but I try to fight it. It comes out in great rolling guffaws and snorts. I'm laughing at myself, the ghost in the reflection of the machine. I laugh and cough and feel sick and spit out a little more bile that's pooling in the sides of my cheek.

"If only you could see me now," I say to the reflection and laugh again. I slip back into unconsciousness and stay there on the floor until Carol comes in to deliver the last of the pills that I'm supposed to take before I go under.

I hear her scream; I think she thinks I'm dead. "I'm not," I try to say but can't. She moves to the phone on my desk and calls one of the doctors. I know this because when I come to again, the doctor is there with an IV drip, poking me. The next time I wake up, I'm lying in the infirmary in the middle of my building staring at the freeze chamber. They poke me with more sharp things, things that would hurt me if I could feel them.

I'm drugged. Everything is happening slowly but in triple-speed, as well. There are people in zip-up plastic suits pulling my clothes off. I let them. I'm the emperor and I have no clothes. I giggle and one of the men in plastic looks at me like I'm crazy.

I hear, *"He's ready."*

I hear the machine turn on. It's loud. I don't fight. I know what's coming. Someone picks me up. I'm naked except for my own plastic pair of underwear. I look down and my body follows my head. The plastic men catch me and one of them says, "Whoa there, fella."

I look over *Fella's* shoulder and I see Carol outside the door, and for a split second I think I see Phil. Smiling old Phil and my brain snaps back into focus. Smiling Phil is holding hands with smiling Janet? No, that's not right.

The plastic men do what they need to do; I don't fight them.

I hear the door to the chamber lock. It's very cold—very very very cold. The air sucks out. *I'm dead*, says my brain. So cold when you're dead. Smiling Phil is holding hands with smiling Janet and I'm in here, so cold. Then I'm dreaming again. But this isn't dreaming.

10.

I'm alive. At least, I think I'm alive and if you think you're alive then I guess it's as good as being alive. I can't hear my heartbeat; I can't feel my lungs, but I know that I'm breathing. There are machines making me breathe. Lack of oxygen is what damages the brain, or lack of oxygen in the blood is what damages the brain. I think. I don't really know. I'm good at code. I'm good at perfect things: lines and strings of letters and numbers, commands that tell other "Things" what to do.

It's white, very white like snow. It was cold when I went in here, and I'm sure this is just my brain trying to dream up some connection, make a pattern and display a picture. It's telling itself to do something, to make something. It's writing code.

I laugh into the vacant white. I'm alone and this is dreaming without being able to dream. This is death. Time is, of course, completely meaningless. There are no seconds, minutes, hours or days. There is just white like a blanket of snow or cotton or milk or marshmallows or whatever else is white. Like an open editor on a screen. Empty. This is death; death is empty. I wish more people knew that. It would make living bearable.

THIS IS THE END

PART TWO

1.

My left eye opens first, then my right—very slowly, just a quick flicker of my eyelids—then they shut again. It's so bright. The next sensation that hits me is that I can hear my heartbeat, not outside of my body; I'm not floating above it like a ghost. I can hear the steady thump-thump-thumping of my heart. First, it's behind my eyes. I don't want to open them again; it's so bright and white, just like the dream I was just having. Then my breathing hits me. I can't hear the machine, but my chest is rising and falling in slow, shallow breaths. I'm alive. I'm alive enough to know that I'm alive, at least. I can feel the tubes connecting me to the machine. My stomach feels emptier than it's ever been. I slowly open my eyes again; this time I squint until I can bear the light. It's not white anymore. The window to the tube I'm in is fogged over.

I move my fingers at first, just enough to try and make a fist, just enough to make an open hand. I have enough room to move my arms a little and I try that out. My legs feel like jello. I'm somewhat seated. Mental facilities seem to be fine. Motor skills are setting in and so is my apparent dizziness.

Inside the tube smells terrible, like a mixture of a hospital and a port-a-potty. Speaking of which, my bladder says it's full. I wait a few seconds and then decide to see if I can move enough to pull off the breathing mask. I hit the foot-thick clear composite window on the door. When I brush it with my arm, it leaves an open spot in the fog. I see the floor.

I start to panic. It's so small in here. I haven't spoken yet. I try to make sound with my mouth but nothing comes out. My eyes are hurting, they go wider. I have to tell myself not to panic. "Don't panic," I say, but it's all internal. And then I ask, "Where the hell is everyone?"

I want to say something out loud. I need to. Maybe they've left me. Maybe they think I'm dead. Didn't I install a failsafe, a button on the inside? Questions. Questions. Questions.

My hands try and move around the nearly invisible seam of the door. I start to panic when I don't feel a lever, latch, handle or button. I have yet to make a sound or move from the waist down. I'm very pale. I feel as if I am going to be sick. I am rebreathing the air I exhale. I will die in here.

The suction cup breathing mask itches. I'm drooling and my chest hurts. I hit something big and white and bulbous and then I hear the door decompress. The vacuum seal releases; a burst of warmer air floods the inside of the tube's chamber. The fog on the window gets thicker—too cold in here, too warm outside. I push forward with every ounce of strength that I can possibly muster; my stomach feels so empty and adrenaline floods my body.

My arms are shaking as I push the door out away from me. It's heavy but the hinges are in good working order; they glide and then I fall out of the machine, slamming into the floor. The mask pulls up and off of my face, over my head with no resistance. I try and brace for the impact, but I'm too weak after pushing, no use of my legs yet.

I slam into the floor and it hurts worse than anything I've ever felt, worse than it should because pain is new again. I'm on the floor and I gag, too much adrenaline not enough food, no liquids. Need liquids.

Isn't this how I got here? I ask myself. My throat still doesn't make a sound—nothing but the heavy breathing of my lungs. I'm naked, save for the plastic pants they put on me before, and covered in something that feels like Vaseline, water and jelly. Something slick and slimy. Little shattered memories stab my brain: the plastic men, the doctors, Phil and Janet standing watching me. They were smiling.

I feel it in my chest, nothing. Am I cured? I had cancer. I reach for the floor to pull myself up, try to stand. I feel my feet. I feel blood entering my feet. I'm looking at my arms; they're so pale. My head begins pounding; my mouth is so dry. I kick out with one leg then another and crawl away from the tube, the machine. My plastic pants are making crinkle-crinkle sounds as I drag myself across the floor. I leave a trail of clear jelly grease slime behind me. There's a table to my right. I reach up and try to pull. My hands are weak and come crashing back on top of my head. I have no hair. I rub my head; it's bald. I have no hair.

I lay down. I curl up into a ball. I begin to shiver. I'm alive, awake and it's so cold. I'm alive and awake and I'm lying on the floor. Then I hear it—my own voice. It's small and quiet at first. But it's mine. I remember it.

"I'm alive," I say though my throat hurts. There's no moisture in my mouth. I say it again and again and again: "I'm alive."

I pass out.

* * *

The second time I wake up is much smoother; it feels normal, almost natural. I'm still cold and my head still feels like it's been used as a soccer ball, but my body is more receptive. I'm able to get up without falling over. I'm still not that steady on my feet but I can stand upright. I brace myself on the corner of the table that I tried to crawl to before.

"Where the fuck is everyone?" I say. I need to use my voice. I need to hear it enough to get used to it again. Everything looks dirty—not filthy, but dusty. I shiver and then start to look around for something that I can put on. There are two lab coats hanging on the wall that appear to be clean. I use the table as a guide and walk myself over to them and put them both on. I'm freezing. I look around for evidence that someone has been here recently to check on me.

There are some forms outlining procedures to take and levels to check on a metallic clipboard. I scan the piece of paper looking for the last date that someone was here and stop when I come to the last entry. I double-check the date. Then I triple-check it to make sure. I leaf through the rest of the documents and try to find something else that would show me that they stopped using this particular form or maybe even paper in general. Nothing.

THIS IS THE END

I look back at the date: one year. And the last time anyone checked on me was roughly six months after I was put in the tube.

"Can't be," I say out loud, still trying to recognize every syllable. I scan the room again; nothing looks out of place, but nothing looks touched either. The power is still on or, at least, the lights are. I pull the piece of paper off the metal clipboard and shove it into the pocket of the outermost lab coat and then pull the inner one shut around me.

"I paid a shit-ton of money to these people and they can't even do their fucking job right..." Then it hits me. I remember Phil standing with Janet again. They were holding hands, and they were smiling. My brain starts to put two and five together and comes up with I-got-fucked.

I look around to see if there is anything else in the room. One last time, anything to make me feel like I'm wrong. Then I look over at the machine. The door is still standing wide open; the breathing mask is flopped on the floor just outside. All the monitors are turned off. The power to the machine was cut for some reason. I blink.

I have to get to my office and find out what the fuck happened. After that, I have some people to find and hurt.

2.

The doors swing open and the motion sensors trip; I hear the click and hum of electricity in the bulbs above me. It takes a few minutes for all of them to flicker on, a few panels stay dark and I wonder where everyone is. There isn't anything to tell me that anyone has been here in quite some time. I look around and, again, like the other room, nothing looks out of place but nothing looks right either. I start walking and the tiled floor under my feet is ice cold.

It's a funny sensation as the blood comes rushing back to my body. I can feel it move through my veins. I feel the pressure in my arms and legs returning; everything is swelling up inside me, back to normal, I guess. Someone was supposed to be watching me 24 hours a day, every day. But the room I'm in right now, I've only been to, conservatively, twice before. Maybe they moved operations up to another floor and have some sort of vid-stream on the room?

No, if that were the case then someone would have seen me by now. This isn't right; none of this is right.

I'm standing here, practically naked and freezing fucking cold and no one is here and Janet and Phil were holding hands. This is a set up. I never should have trusted him.

I stop in front of the elevator doors, push the button and wait. Nothing. I push the button again, wait a few more seconds and then realize that there isn't any power to the elevators. The lights are off; the little digital screen that should show you the floor you are on is black and silent. I turn around and look at the room; by law there has to be an entrance to the stairs here somewhere. Why has the power to the elevators been cut? Jesus Christ, I bet they stole my money, closed this fucking place down and then cut all the power to kill me.

That can't be right. Why would the rest of the building have power? Why would the lights come on?

"Solar membranes," I say to nobody. "The windows, all of them, have solar membranes."

It helped sell the feature to other companies; the whole building is running on solar right now. It's not that there isn't any power, just not enough. They were originally a backup plan until we could install our own grid. They were never meant to be the sole powersource for the whole damn building, just a reserve for the server banks. I need to see the outside. I need to get to a set of windows.

The entrance to the stairs is off to the right. The floor is starting to become colder than my feet and it's making my toes ache. My stomach turns over a few times. I need to eat something soon, something with a little substance or else I'm going to pass out again. My hands are shaky when I reach the push bar of the security door that leads to the stairwell. It opens with ease and I look up and then down. I'm on the third floor, only three more to go until I can get to my office. Grabbing hold of the handrail, I begin to pull myself up, one foot at a time. The emergency lights are the only lights in the narrow space; big, red exit signs throw just enough light on the floor to make it accessible, and my eyes instantly feel better.

I make it up one flight and have to sit down on the landing. I haven't moved in a year. Take that and couple it with the fact that I haven't had anything but medication, and you get a very weak and tired man. My hand goes to my head and I rub the smoothness. I used to have a pretty good head of hair, but I guess the chemo and the other treatments along with the freezing process pretty much killed that. I can deal with baldness. The skin on my hands and arms shines in the low light; my whole body is pale enough to glow in the dark. After I take a few deep breaths, I pull myself up to the handrail and look into the glass opening of the security door in front of me.

I can't remember what we had on the fourth floor; I think it was Research and Development, maybe it was accounting? The lights are all off. The portal is black; I try the handle and it feels like there's something blocking it when I try to push it open. Standing on my tiptoes, I look down and try to see if there's something in the way. Why would there be something in the way?

Fuck it; I need to get to my office. I need to figure this out. But first I need clothes and coffee and food. God, I would kill for a cup of coffee right now. I stop trying to look through the little square window and keep moving. Hand over hand, it feels like I'm climbing Everest. I keep moving until I get past the landing for the fifth floor; the landing just above me reads a big 6, and then I see the door to my floor and smile.

I put my hand on the handle and push down. It clicks but doesn't move and for a few seconds I freak out. "Maybe they locked me in the building." I push forward a little harder and it opens. I smile wider. I missed my office.

I want a triple espresso. I want my comfortable, expensive, tailored clothing. A shower. Food—God, I'm going to order so much stupid food and I'm not even going to finish it, just throw it away. I want to take a shit. Then I want to find these assholes and do something very bad to them.

I move into the main portion of my lobby and even before the lights begin to come on, I can see the outline of my couch and Carol's desk. The small trace of ambient light gleams off the polished doors to my sanctuary. I hear the click of energy flowing into tubes and diodes as the room is flooded with piercingly bright light. I instantly wish they hadn't turned on.

It takes a few seconds to figure out what it is I'm looking at. It takes a few seconds for my brain to categorize, to put the picture together: the colors, the smell, the bone-grey and blood-like dirt and shell casings bright as crushed copper roaches. It takes a few seconds for me to figure this all out.

When I do, I turn around and dry heave on the door.

3.

My brain turns around in circles.
I'm in the landing again.
I'm rocking back and forth.
I don't want to go back in there.
I don't like my office anymore.
This has to be a joke.

This is a cruel joke that Phil and Janet played on me. Maybe, maybe Robert had them killed; maybe I've been framed. I don't want to go backing there. Sitting here in the dark, the floor is cold and hard on my ass, even with the plastic diaper and lab coats.

Then I hear it. Something moved behind me. I look at the wall in front of me; the lights are still on in the lobby and I can see someone move past the opening of the window.

I watch the shadow on the wall in front of me. This is a huge joke. I launch myself up and turn around. There's nothing there. I look into the window, scan left to right, and still nothing. The lights flicker out making the window a black rectangular hole again. I slip myself down off the tips of my toes to the cold concrete, look down and shake my head.

Maybe I'm losing it. I haven't had anything to eat yet; I feel shaky enough as it is and the dry heaving didn't help much. I'm just seeing things. Then I hear something faint from the other side of the door, like breathing but it's quiet. I bend down and put my ear to the door. I can't hear much but there's definitely something making noise on the other side of the door.

I bet this is part of the joke. I bet they're all standing around waiting for me to open the door again.

"*We totally got you,*" they'll say and I'll feel like an asshole and everyone will laugh and then I'll fire them all. They'll all laugh again and so will I, because I'm not joking. Then it will get very silent. I will continue to laugh.

More noise is coming from the other side of the door; I hear something that sounds like shuffling or scratching, like someone's dragging something across the floor. There's no way they are locking me in the fucking stairwell. Something hits the door with such force that I stumble back. I look at the door. It happens again. I look into the window.

The lights turn on and I nearly fall down the stairs. The door bursts open and I move backwards. The silhouette of the man standing on the landing doesn't look right. I try to figure it out; looking from left to right, he's missing an arm, his right arm. His face is grey and he's missing an arm.

"This isn't fucking funny," I scream at him.

He says nothing. He comes at me. He's dragging his left leg; he's missing his left foot.

"Cut the fucking shit," I yell at him but he doesn't stop. I'm ready though. I've had enough of this. He stumbles after taking another step with his stump and comes crashing down the stairs missing me completely and slams into the landing below. I grab the door before it has a chance to close and pull it shut behind me.

"Fuck you, asshole. I hope you're seriously hurt. And don't expect me to pay any of the fucking medical." I begin to say something further but realize that, as I'm looking at the man in the suit lying on the landing below, he's getting up.

He's crooked. Men aren't supposed to be crooked like that. I pull the door closed. This isn't right. He makes his way back up the steps; one at a time, he pulls himself up towards the door, then the window. My grip goes tighter on the handle, pulling it impossibly close to me. I start looking for the lock.

The door slams again but this time the sound is accompanied by shattering glass; I pull my head up to look but don't realize that his arm is through the window until it's too late. He grabs my throat. He lets out a moan. Hot, fetid breath hits me in the face. My stomach bottoms out again and I want to retch.

I can't breath. He's grabbing me; I have to let go of the door. His hands are so cold, digging into my neck. I can't scream.

I smash the door into him. His grip breaks and pulls away from my throat, leaving burning finger marks along the sides of my neck. He falls back down the steps and I hear him smack into the landing again. Pulling the door back closed, I look around. There's a gun lying on the couch next to man that doesn't have a top to his head anymore. A Bible is on the floor.

I run to the couch and grab the gun. I have fired a gun five times in my life which was the sum total amount of times I had to go to a firing range so that I could carry the pistol in my car. I wouldn't say I'm the best, but I know how one works.

From behind me I hear the door open. I turn around, the man is there. He's wearing what looks like the remains of a suit and what's left of him is big, muscular. He looks like he could have been on my security detail. His face is tattered and ragged. I can't make out his features to know for sure. He's moving towards me, pulling his dead appendages behind him. His clubfoot makes him unsteady; his left arm is pealed back and covered in shattered glass and scars. There's no blood.

I pull the gun up on him and check quickly to make sure the safety is off and pull the trigger.

Click.

I look down at the gun then back up to him; he's still coming, drool or fluids of some kind drip out of the corner of his jaw. I would say mouth, but that's not really a way to describe it.

I pull the trigger again and again there's another click.

Fuck.

He lunges at me. He hits me. We roll.

He tries to bite my face; I shove my hands into his neck to push him back and it feels like I'm grabbing at sausages. His neck collapses and I feel spine. Black, sticky fluid begins to run down my arms, covering them to my elbows. The smell is nearly unbearable. My throat and abdomen are gagging in tandem, sending waves of heaves up my body like water. The man clicks his teeth at me, clacks his jaws open and closed. I squeeze harder until I take hold of what I know has to be his spinal column. I turn and pull and then I hear a very uncomfortable thick crack.

His eyes roll back into his head and he slumps down on top of me. I push him off. I roll away. I'm covered in black to my shoulders.

I scramble away, looking for something to wipe my arms off with. I see Carol's legs sticking out from behind her desk. I look when I know I shouldn't. She's wearing a skirt and from her feet to her stomach she looks pristine; from her stomach up there is an empty hole. She doesn't have a face anymore because she doesn't have a head. I pull at her skirt and it comes off; I wipe my hands off and throw the skirt back on top of her.

Leaning against the door to my office, scanning the room, I can feel my body start to shake. The adrenaline dump is making the room spin. I brace my body with the corner of her desk and pull myself to the door controls.

"Come on, come on, fucking work." I say to the finger scanner as I lay my index finger on the little glass. I can see the laser inside is still working, see the little crisscross of red light on my finger tip.

"Come on," I scream at the screen. Then I hear the lock click behind me. The door to my office opens and I crawl inside and wait to hear it close again. The room springs to life, power comes back on. Lights flicker, screens load. I hear computers boot up. I'm shaking uncontrollably now, every muscle in my body is tensing and releasing all at once.

I look around and see the room spinning. Then I see the barrel of a gun. I hear a click. I see boots.

"Who the fuck are you, and how did you get in here?" asks someone—sounds like a woman. The barrel of a gun is very cold. Never knew that before. I can't answer back, I'm so tired. I look over and there are more feet.

"Help me. Please?" I manage to ask. My throat is closing up, can't stop the shaking.

Someone kicks me in the head.

Thank you.

4.

"Who are you?" asks the woman who held the gun to my head earlier. She's standing in front of me and I'm strapped to a chair, arms and legs bound tight. My left eye is incredibly swollen; I can barely see out of it. Boots kicked me in the head.

"Who the fuck are *you*?" I ask back, and then regret saying anything as her open hand slams against my face. *Sometimes you're the windshield; sometimes you're the fly*, says my brain. I shake my head and try to focus again.

"I'm the one asking questions here, so I'm gonna ask you again: who are you, how did you get in here, and what are you doing here?"

She's not very pretty. Hard lines mark the corners of her mouth—"Frown lines," Janet used to call them. Her eyes are cold and hard. She has short hair pulled back in a ponytail. Her clothes look like they fell off the back of a truck bound for a survivalist dyke convention. I run my tongue over my lips trying not to laugh at my own joke and taste blood.

"I need water. Please, some water and then I'll tell you," I say back and brace for another slamming fist. To my surprise I get a bottle of water with a straw instead of another smack.

"Here," she says and I take a small sip. The water is cold and tastes like blood mixed with nothing, but it helps. There's another person standing next to her. He's skinny and wearing similar clothing. He has guns.

He looks just as tired as she does; his eyes are just as cold, black and empty. She pulls the straw and bottle away from me and I try to smile the five thousand dollar smile at her. I don't think it's going to work. I don't think my smile is worth that much anymore.

"I own this building," I begin to say but Skinny cuts me off.

"Nobody owns buildings anymore, asshole," he says but she puts up her hand and Skinny obeys.

Good. Now I know who's in charge. I look at Skinny and make sure he knows I'd like to snap his neck. I probably couldn't, at least not in this condition. But still, it's the thought that counts.

"Can I finish?" I ask them but really, I'm still staring at Skinny. Nobody moves. I don't get another hand in the face. Skinny looks the other way, out towards the windows.

"Good. Like I was saying my name is Jeff and I own this building. Maybe you've heard of me: Jeff Sorbenstein? I was *Time* magazine's Man of the Year last year."

I see her face soften; Skinny is still looking out the window, completely *not* paying attention. Then he spits on the floor.

"Hey, what the fuck, do I come over to your house and spit on your floor?" I say to his back.

He turns back to me and laughs and then comes in real close. His breath is hot and smells terrible.

"Listen," he says, "for all intents and purposes, champ, this *is* my home so if I want to spit, shit or anything else on the fucking floor, then I fucking will. Got it?" Then he turns around and looks back at the woman and asks, "Right, Kel?"

The woman is staring at me like she just put two and five together and now it's her turn to get fucked. She's probably thinking about how much shit she's going to be in or, more likely, how much money she can get out of me. I try to smile at her again but she's fumbling with her holster, then she's pointing her gun at my head.

"You're a monster; you're the fucking monster that did this," she says in a whisper, eyes wide.

Great, just my luck, anti-technology freaks. My building has been overrun by anti-tech heads.

I look up at her and ask, "What?"

Her hand is shaking; her finger is resting on the side of the trigger. She's pushing the gun into my forehead—leaving a mark, a small circle less than the size of a dime is being slowly drilled into the middle of my head and I'm about to die for the second time in my life. Skinny looks surprised; he's trying to ask her questions and I close my eyes, waiting for the sound, waiting for the heat of the bullet.

"Kel, what the fuck are you doing?" asks Skinny. I can hear the shock in his voice. Something's not right. I open my eyes and Skinny is looking at her like she's completely lost it, like he's the sane one. She's the one I have to talk to, try and reason with. Jesus, I got cancer, froze myself, got screwed over by my lawyer and ex-wife who then left me for dead and now I have to deal with this.

"He's the one that did this," she says back to him. Her eyes are rimming with shock and tears.

Skinny looks confused; he glances at me then back out the window and then, as if an actual light bulb went off in his head, he finally figures out what she's trying to tell him. He lunges at me; his eyes are filled with rage.

She screams his name as we tumble backwards onto the floor. I think she says "Scott"—I'm not sure. Skinny is mashing his fist into my head and his hands feel like cinder blocks.

"I'm gonna smash your fucking brains in, asshole," he's yelling into my face—hot, dirty breath. I still have no idea what it is that they're talking about. I try to tell them but every time I open my mouth, another of his fists hits me. She moves in to pull him off me and I don't know if I'm thankful or not. I can't tell anymore.

"Scott, stop," she says pulling him off of me. Trails of spit and blood follow his hands; he breaks free and comes back at me.

"Scott, Goddamnit, that's an order," she yells and he stops as if he's on autopilot. Then he stands up straight and faces her.

"You're not in charge anymore, Kel. Remember? No more orders. That's what we said when we came in here."

She bites her lip and looks like a child and says, "I know, Scott, but if it is really him then he doesn't know."

Skinny looks confused again. "How can he not know?" he asks.

She looks over at me like she's checking my face, making sure I'm telling the truth, then looks back to him. "Because he froze himself before everything happened."

Skinny doesn't understand and neither do I, but I'm glad he's not trying to ram his fist into my skull through my face. She was just going to blow my head off, now she's saving me from having my head smashed in. I don't get it. Now my right eye feels swollen; I think he broke my nose.

"You were just gonna blow his head off," he says back to her.

She shakes her head. "No. I lost my cool. It's just...I was...I lost my cool," she says through thickening tears. I try to look around but my eyelids feel too heavy. Skinny moves in to hug her; she wipes away the tears from her eyes. They move apart but there's a connection here that isn't just on the surface—have to remember that.

"What? What did I do?" I ask. My voice sounds frail and distant. They turn to me and pull me back up and then push my chair towards the windows, slamming me into it. I try to focus. My head feels like it's full of oatmeal. The light outside is incredibly bright, like a blanket of grey. I look out towards the skyline. I force my eyes open and see the world for the first time since I woke up.

Low-hanging cloud cover isn't really cloud cover; the sky is blue above the haze. It's smoke. Huge billows of black, white and grey smoke waft through the corridors of the city. Cars in the street crisscross lanes as if they were just left to crash. Doors hang open, bodies lay just outside them. Military vehicles are smashed and broken. There are several metal fences, crowd control barricades, scattered around, and some are overturned and left like skeletons. I see people walking, stumbling around. Some of them have arms and legs that look broken, crooked like the man in the lobby. Some of them look like they just woke up and went off to work, but there's still something off about them.

The streetlights are all out. Black and white bags line the sidewalks and streets; they're bulky, lumpy. They have bodies in them. The dead are dumped and rotting. The sky is blue and the dead line the street and the cars are abandoned and the sky is on fire. The sun is dim and yellow; mixed into the haze of the smoke it looks evil. I focus in on some of the people in the street, walking, falling, searching, looking—their faces are wrong. The world is wrong. The world is burning.

The familiar outline of both the Terminal Tower and Key Tower look like stubbed cigars, charred and brown. Public Square is full of broken, crooked, bloody, grey-skinned people. My city is burning; my city is dead.

"What happened?" I ask, still staring out the window, still trying to understand what it is that I'm seeing.

"You," says the woman named Kel. She moves towards Skinny—Scott—whatever. They're standing behind me now, holding each other. I can see the outline of their joined shape in the glass of the window. I look out and see the world, my world.

"Let me go," I say and Skinny laughs.

"No way, asshole," he says.

"I need to know how this happened," I say back, but I can't stop looking out across the city, my city.

"We just told you," he says, then starts in on me with something else, I cut him off.

"Do you want to eat hot food tonight?" I say but nobody answers back; I can feel the hesitation in the air. They're considering it.

"I can route the power from the solar panels to just this room. Right now it's being used up by keeping the base systems on: lights, magnetic locks, *et cetera*. I can reroute it all to come in here and we can have hot water, hot food and internet."

Skinny laughs again. I haven't heard from Kel yet. She's thinking about it though. I can't see her face, but I know she's not that stupid.

"There's no more internet, dude," says Skinny.

I crane my head around to look back at him. "I am the fucking internet, *dude*. Every website, blog, micro blog, tweet, news site, feed, vid-feed, everything—it's all cached on the main servers that are housed in the middle of this room. I have to know what happened. Untie me, please."

"What's going to happen if those magnetic locks unlock and those things get in here, huh? Did you think about that?"

"I can route enough power to keep those online," I say.

He starts to object again but Kel cuts him off and says, "Okay."

She moves to untie me. The knots around my hands loosen and I immediately feel better. I move to untie the ones at my feet and then stand up. Before I turn around I hear the gun. I turn around slowly and Kel is there. I stare at the gun again.

"If you so much as move in a way that makes me think you're fucking us over, I will shoot you. Do you understand?" she says.

I nod and say, "Yes," to make sure she knows that I understand, completely.

"Good, now get to work." She motions with the gun towards my desk then lets her arm come down; I nod again slowly and move. I sit down in my chair. It feels good, even with knowing that one wrong move means that I'll probably be dead before I can blink. Just the thought of sitting behind my desk again makes me feel alive. I smile.

"Okay," I whisper to the touchscreens as they blink to life. "Here we go."

* * *

It takes me three hours to route all of the power that's been sitting in the backup generators to my office. The sun is going down now and I'm still at my desk. My hands feel like they're cramping up and my back is killing me.

I haven't eaten anything yet, but I did get up once to make some coffee. My stomach feels like its eating itself alive and I'm fairly nauseous, but I don't want to stop until I have everything done and uploaded. There isn't anything left in the fridge food-wise, but I'm pretty sure there's enough canned stuff down in the cafeteria to last us a while. It was well-stocked and probably locked down the minute the building went dark.

I tell them about the cafeteria and they talk about how they're going to go about getting there. I position one of the screens so that they can look at it and pull up a map of the building showing the fastest routes and the video feeds from all of the surveillance cameras that are still intact.

Later, when the sun starts to go down, we decide to keep the lights dim enough for us to see each other and where were going in the rooms. Anything more and it'll probably attract attention that we don't want. I ask them about the outbreak—what they know of it, at least. They don't tell me much, but I can't believe what I'm hearing. It sounds like a movie. I begin to pull in the first of the large cached files that'll have the backups I need.

They take turns watching me. First it's Kel and then it's Scott. We don't talk. This is to say they don't talk to me, at least not enough to be considered a conversation. They ask me if I'm sure that there's enough power to split between everything that I'm doing and the magnetic locks and I say, "I'm sure."

The building's been storing solar power in banks of generators large enough to power small countries in the sub-sub-basement. The only thing we really have to worry about is the diesel backups. But since the building hasn't been running full-steam for almost a year, there should be enough to get us through at least a year, or so I hope. I don't tell them the last part.

I look down and the screen reads out the time: 5:55. I look up again and stare out the window and time has no meaning. It's completely dark now and the only light in the place is the white glow of my monitors.

Bringing the lights back up is easier than I thought. Getting the right amount of light to see in but that can't be seen by whatever those things in the street are, is much more difficult. I hunker back down over the screens and start tapping in commands to pull up the last date that there was anything updated on the main servers. The lights flicker a bit making them both jump.

"What the fuck?" asks Scott. He's pointing another gun at me. I wave dismissively with my right hand.

"I just brought my main servers back online again, just a small hiccup," I say back to him. He's sitting on the chair that Rob threw me into and I smile. I bet Rob got away. It's getting easier to work with a gun pointed at me. For the first half hour or so, when I was trying to really concentrate on not screwing up the sequences, it was a little distracting, but now I don't even notice. It's just there.

I pull up the last of large format files and ping in. The screen to my right blazes to life with my sign in then starts pulling up every feed that went out in the last year. I make sure to do an external save to a new set of ghost servers and then wave my hand in front of the screen to make it sleep. Later.

I get up and move out from behind my desk and stretch.

I say to them, "I need to eat something, but first I am making another pot of coffee and taking a shower. When I'm done I am going down to cafeteria and getting food. Are you coming with me?" They look at each other and then back to me as if I've just said something in Hebrew.

Scott starts first. "Do you know what those things are out there, man? They're fucking zombies, as in eat-our-ass-for-dinner zombies."

"I already pulled up all of the videos from the cafeteria and the floor plan. You've had enough time to figure something out. If not, I don't care. I'm going," I say, cutting him off.

Kel shakes her head. "Okay, we'll go, but if you—"

I cut her off too. I'm sick and tired of this; I'm starting to feel like me again. "It's my building, my food and if you want any of it then you'll come with me. If not, then you can go get your own food by yourselves later. And spare me the 'I'll shoot you' routine. I get it."

Scott gets up like he's going to hit me again. I stop him.

"Really? You're gonna hit the guy that could easily fuck your whole day up by letting those—whatever they are—into the building?"

Scott sits back down and says, "Fuck you, asshole."

I turn back to Kel. "Look, you have the guns, but I have the controls. You got it?"

She nods her head, still not sure of where I'm going with this speech, probably kicking herself mentally for letting me out of the chair.

"We're a democracy now," I say to both of them. Scott pouts and mumbles something that sounds like "whatever."

"So that means that right now you need me and I need you. So we share," I say and wait for some kind of push back, but Scott just keeps pouting.

Kel nods her head again and says, "Agreed."

I move towards my kitchen. The last time I was here I was lying on the floor in my own filth and puke. I look down at the coffee pot and then down to my plastic pants and the lab coat outfit. Not much has changed. I put a new pot of coffee on and then move back out towards the main office area. Scott is fumbling with a lighter and a cigarette butt that looks like it's been his last cigarette butt for years. Nobody should have to smoke like that.

I say, "Hey," and they both turn around. I point towards my desk. "Bottom desk drawer: there are cartons and lighters. No menthol, just regular. I don't know how fresh they are but it's better than that thing, I'm sure."

His eyes go wide. I move up the stairs to my bedroom and grab some clothing and then head back down and into the bathroom. Scott's already smoking; Kel is lighting up as I come down.

She nods her head and I'm pretty sure that means thanks. I nod back and say, "Save me some," then go into the bathroom.

The water isn't as hot as I would like it to be. I figure the instant hots haven't been up and running in at least nine months, but right now it's the best shower I have taken in my entire life, ever.

When I come out, I'm dressed; my skin is still incredibly pale, even against the white shirt I'm wearing. The suit looks stupid compared to their gear but I was never one for the outdoors so I don't really own anything that's utilitarian. The whole office is bathed in milky-blue bands of cigarette smoke and smells like coffee. It almost feels normal.

"You're a little dressed up to get food," says Scott. One of my American Spirits is nestled in the corner of his mouth. I look down again at my outfit, nod and say, "Yeah."

I've lost a lot of weight. I wasn't very big before being frozen, but I would say that, looking down at how roomy the perfectly tailored suit and shirt is, I've lost at least twenty pounds.

Kel breaks the silence by pulling back the slide on her pistol. She gets up and then asks if everyone is ready. Scott does the same and nods back to her; they look at me. I sit down in my chair and put on my shoes and then get up. The room wants to spin but I stop it and say, "As I'll ever be."

"Do you have anything that you can use if we run into any of them?" she asks.

I think about it. "No, that's why you're going," I answer back.

She shrugs and we move back to the screen that has the layout and camera feeds. I point at the monitor and flip the layout of the cafeteria around. The cameras follow the screen and the feeds update to reflect the new positions. There isn't any immediate movement in any of the hallways or cafeteria, nothing that looks like it's potentially life threatening, at least. But then again, the thing from before didn't make a move until it knew I was around. I key in the command to bring up the lights in the cafeteria. There aren't any windows so I go full blast; it looks like it did before I was frozen: trays neatly stacked, utensils waiting to be used, napkins in their holders. The stainless steel of the kitchen has a muted glow, but other than that, it looks like a frozen moment in time. I guess it is now.

I wait a few seconds before tapping the screen and picking the hallways that make up the fastest route between here and there, nothing moving in those either. I turn to them and then map it out, including floor numbers and how we can get there from here.

"It's just a few floors, and it doesn't look like anything's in there, so it should be fairly easy," I say to Kel.

"You're the one who doesn't have a weapon," she says looking back at me.

I look out at the door to the lobby and the image of what's out there—Carol and the other bodies, the man I killed earlier—all of it hits me. I swallow and then turn back to them. "Just remember, anything happens to me you don't get back in here," I say more for my own benefit than theirs.

Scott laughs and moves towards the door, arm outstretched and ready. "Anything happens to you and we're gonna cut your fucking hand off so we *can* get back in here."

I open the doors and we move out in to the lobby. The crooked man from before is still there where he slumped over after I broke his neck. Dirty brown blood stains are everywhere, the black ooze that was all over my arms is pooled around the area of his neck that I shoved my hands into. I shudder and then see the pistol on the floor. I grab it and move over to the body of the headless man on the couch.

"What are you doing?" asks Kel.

I stick my hand inside his suit jacket where the holster should be, then move my way around his chest to the other side and pull out the clip and check it.

"Bullets," I say back to her.

"You know how to handle a gun?" she asks, more surprise than actual concern in her voice.

I'm not the smoothest but I pull back the slide, pop the clip in and hit the release. "Yeah, I'm good," I say. Scott moves back towards where we're standing.

"Hey, you guys wanna hurry it up or—" he says before he notices the gun. "Who said you could have a gun?"

"It's my building, I get a gun," I say back to him, trying to make sure he gets it. He shrugs his shoulders and then moves back out to the front.

"Whatever, just means I don't have to babysit your pale ass. Now lead away, big man," he says.

"You're welcome for the cigarettes," I mumble as I step in front of him to open the door to the stairs. I disabled the emergency lights to pull as much power as I could to the servers and the office, and I wish I hadn't now. The stairwell is an immense black void and we stand in the door opening and stare into it for what seems like minutes. I move in to the darkness and let it swallow me. I hear the other two follow, and then the door closes behind us completely.

"Did anyone remember to bring a flashlight?" I ask. I move down to the first step, hands fumbling to find the rail in the dark. The broken glass from the door's window makes little grinding, crunching noises as they follow. There's a click from behind me and I tense up; I'm still waiting for one of them to put a bullet into me. They have what they want.

A thin beam of white light cuts through the black stairwell and lights the way down. The broken glass sparkles like diamond dust, shadows take on an infinite blackness in contrast to the pale LEDs and we continue to move. We move slowly down the steps towards the second floor.

"I liked this better in the dark," I say into the emptiness. Nobody answers back or disagrees.

5.

"Holy shit, that's a lot of food," says Scott as he moves into pantry. I follow behind and Kel stays in the doorway. She hands me her backpack and we start filling it with as much as we possibly can. Scott starts handing me can after can, everything from green beans to asparagus, sliced and whole potatoes, corn and carrots. There isn't much in the way of meat, we passed that freezer on our way into the back of the kitchen and decided that if the smell was that bad on the outside then it's not even worth going inside. There are a couple of cans of chicken and tuna; I grab some peanut butter and throw that in, as well.

We fill up her bag first then I try to pick up the bag, test its weight, and I can't. I'm feeling very weak. I slide it over to Scott and he removes his pack and trades it for the full one, lifting it easily onto his back.

"Get as much as we can. We don't know if we'll get another chance to come back here or not," says Kel from the doorway. She's scanning the kitchen, looking for signs of anything not us.

"You know what I really would like?" asks Scott, and I don't answer, mainly because I didn't know this was the talking portion of the trip. He keeps going as though I answered anyway. "A fucking beer," he says with a smile.

"You do realize that there was enough liquor upstairs to get you blind drunk," I answer back, pulling another can of mixed vegetables down from the shelf in front of me.

"Yeah, I saw that, but I don't drink liquor," he says handing me another can of sweet potatoes. "Know your limits, I say. Beer? Beer I'm good with; I just can't handle liquor."

"Huh," I say back to him, but I'm not really paying attention. It's getting harder to focus on what I'm doing. Then I see it. A whole storage shelf of brightly packaged, infinitely delicious-looking cupcakes, orange cake, chocolate cake, strawberry frosted cupcakes, everything. I grab a box and tear it open, then the packaging, and then I tear into the cupcakes. The first bite makes me feel as if I've just had a religious experience; the second bite makes me feel like I've transcended religion and become one with the cosmos. I smash two more into my mouth before I notice that they are both staring at me.

"What?" I say, but they just stare.

"You freeze yourself for a year and go without food and see if you're not fucking starving for a cupcake when you come out," I say back.

Then I hear Kel make a noise. She's laughing. Hard, too, and trying not to show it. She turns her head and brings her hand up to her face to stifle it. I turn to Scott and he looks at me and then starts laughing, too. I look down and my hands are covered in destroyed chocolate cupcake; there's frosting and creamy insides all over my hands. I can only imagine what my face looks like.

"Dude," says Scott, "did you forget how to chew when you were on ice?"

I look around and then decide to wipe my hands off on the wall of the pantry.

They laugh for a few more seconds. It sounds good to hear laughter. We finish packing the bag and I slide this one over to Kel; she shoulders the pack easily while I look out the door. The sugar from the cupcakes buzzes through my body making me feel as if I'm going a mile a minute. She taps me on the shoulder and I jump. She steps back and asks if I'm ready.

"Yeah, but there's one more thing I want to check before we leave, okay?" I say back to her. She tries not to smile at me; I still have cupcake smashed onto the sides of my face.

"Is it absolutely necessary?" she asks.

"Yeah," I say looking over at Scott and then add, "I can go by myself, though." I point to the cooler on the other side of the kitchen. I expect her to say no, but instead I get a "Make it quick."

I run over to the other side of the kitchen; the gun is in the front of my pants and it keeps jabbing me in the bladder. I need to pee again, which is insane because I've barely had enough to drink to make me want to pee again. I reach the cooler and pull open the door and go inside, grab what I need and come back out holding two six-packs of Budweiser. Scott nearly drops the cans of black-eyed peas he was carrying.

"Is there more in there?" he asks me.

I nod and say, "All the beer you could ever want to drink."

He walks slowly towards and then right around me, dropping the cans of peas to the ground and disappearing into the cooler. I move back to where Kel is standing.

She shakes her head at me and says, "You know you've just made a big mistake, right?"

"No, I don't, but it's the end of the fucking world. Let him have a beer," I say with a shrug.

"It's not gonna be just *one* beer," she says back to me, the slightest hint of annoyance under the words as if she knows how Scott is going to react and it's not going to be pretty.

I turn to her and ask her sharply, "Does it matter?" She doesn't reply.

From within the cooler we hear a yell, a primal scream that makes us both jump and go for our guns. But it's not a panicked *please come get me, I'm in danger* yell. It's the sound of triumph, a yell of victory. Scott comes out a few minutes later with several four-packs of Guinness and a six-pack of Labatt Blue pint cans in one hand and an open pint of Murphy's Stout in the other. He moves towards me and he already stinks of beer.

"Right now, you're all right. Upstairs you'll be the asshole monster who ended the world, but right now, you're all right," he says and then smiles at me and shotguns the rest of the Murphy's. He crushes the can and tosses it over his shoulder towards the floor.

"Are you two ready, or do you want to make any more noise that might bring some of them in here?" asks Kel, who's already making her way towards the double doors that lead out of the kitchen. Scott opens another pint can and begins to drink heavily. I follow behind him carrying the other two six-packs.

* * *

We move back out through the silent cafeteria and into the stairwell, climbing the four flights of stairs is easy when you don't have another thirty or forty pounds of canned food on your back, so I have the flash light and the lead. Scott has already killed an entire Guinness four-pack and started in on the Labatt, leaving a trail of crushed cans in his wake. Now I understand what Kel was trying to say to me before. Scott is very annoying when he's drunk, definitely more talkative, but very annoying.

We decide to stop on the fifth floor landing for a minute and rest. I hold the flashlight in my hands and it makes a cone of light up towards the ceiling.

"So," says Scott, "why did you freeze yourself?"

I start to think of the answer but before I can open my mouth Kel answers for me.

"He had cancer. He wanted to freeze himself so that one day, when they found some kind of cure for cancer, they could wake him up, cure him," then she looks up at me from the steps she's sitting on. "Am I right?"

I nod and say, "Yes," and then add my own question to Scott's. "For terrorists, you sure know a lot about me. What you were looking to get from me?"

Kel looks at me like I just said something else in Hebrew. Scott laughs again.

"Are you shitting me? Dude, you seriously think we're terrorists?" asks Scott, almost doubled over with joy, finishing off the Labatt pint.

"What are you guys then, if you're not anti-tech heads?" I ask.

Kel answers this one, too.

"You're looking at Sergeant Kelly Pitts and this is Corporal Scott Stanton. And, to our knowledge, we are the last of the United States National Guard, possibly the entire Army, maybe the world. Give or take." They throw mock salutes. Skinny Scott's is way off and he pours most of his beer out of the can. Kel's is crisp and practiced, right on as if she were on duty. The finality of her words hits me in my chest; my heart seems to literally sink in my body.

"How did you guys get into my office then?" I ask.

Kel stands up with the help of the handrail and then offers her hand to Scott. I get up and we move towards the door to my lobby.

"It's a long story, but the CliffsNotes version is that we were on our way to pick you up," she says while pushing the door to the lobby open. I move forward and click off the flashlight. The sudden smell of decaying bodies makes my eyes water.

"Why?" I ask back. I put my finger on the scanner for the door, anxious to get back inside the purified air of my office. It clicks open with the familiar hiss of the magnetic release.

"Come on, it's a long story," she says again as she moves past me and into the office.

Scott follows her, but before we can both move any further in, he turns flashes me a smile and then stops and grabs me by the neck and shoulder, pulls me close and says, "Remember, we're back up here. Now you're a monster again."

"Yeah, that's what you keep saying," I say back to him. His breath smells worse than before, like stale cigarettes and warm beer. I pull my face away but can't escape it.

"Remember, you're a monster," he says again, and then adds a long, throaty *rawr* and starts laughing.

I look back at the dead and I'm not sure that I don't believe him.

6.

We make chicken, rice and green beans on my stove; Scott jumps in and grabs enough for two people before Kel and I can fill our plates.

He's gone through the majority of beer that he brought with him and has already started to get to work on the Budweiser six-packs I had liberated. We inhale the food, literally. I take it easy on the first plate, but after the rice and chicken hits my stomach and I manage to keep it down, I begin to eat like I can't stop. After my third plate I want to make more but decide against it. There wasn't that much left in the pantry and Kel is technically right, we don't know when we're going to go back and restock. After we eat I make another pot of coffee. It stops and I pour myself a generous half of a cup, then I make my way for the bar and pour at least four fingers' worth of Jameson 18-year into the other half of the cup and take a long drink.

The liquor hits my full stomach and makes me want to sit down. I move towards my desk and flick the screens on with my hand. The craving starts to build seconds later, and at first I can fight it off with just logging on, but when Scott lights up his cigarette, the pressure's just too much and I pull the drawer with my cigarettes open. I used to demand that there be at least ten cartons of cigarettes in my desk at all times.

It looks like Scott has taken two and Kel probably one, which leaves me with roughly seven cartons to last the entire end of the world. I pull out a pack from one of the already open cartons, slam the bottom end of the pack on my palm a couple of times and then peel off the cellophane and take a long inhale.

"Goddamn, that's a good smell," I say, even the faintest hint of lighting up is setting off receptors that have long been dormant in my brain. I take one of the disposable lighters out of the package and flick my wrist to get out a cigarette.

"You really think you should smoke?" asks Scott.

I look over at him and he's smiling drunk at me.

"Why," I ask him back while lighting up. I take a small drag and inhale, letting muscle memory take over. It's still feels good. Then I cough and cough until I think the room is going to spin. I see little explosions of red and blue and sparkles as my lungs rebel against the thick, delicious smoke.

"Probably because you have cancer, or whatever," says Scott.

I keep coughing and Kel asks if I'm going to be okay. I give her thumbs up and take another swig off my coffee, completely forgetting that I put the Jameson in it. It takes another five minutes for me to return to anything resembling regular breathing patterns. I stub out the cigarette and decide to try again later. Scott is in the chair again, looking out towards the windows. The only lights in the city are the fires scattered about on the horizon and the moon and stars. I tap into the mainframe and it gives me a read out on the outside temperature. It's springtime again, but I'm surprised to see that the temperature reads 55.

"You know what would make this night better?" says Scott as he looks from me over to Kel. She shakes her head and I pretend that I'm not listening.

He stands up and stretches, then says, "Fucking video games."

He goes into the bathroom and I'm left looking at the last remnants of the internet that are waiting for me on the screen; three huge files that have everything that happened up to the very last ping in from whatever computer, wherever that was. A time capsule of the end of days is staring me in the face, but I don't want to open it yet; I don't think I'm ready to know. I turn my focus back to Kel, who is looking out at the dying city and smoking a cigarette of her own.

"So, you never said why you were coming to get me or how you got in here," I say to her back. I see her faint reflection in the window. She smiles and starts to tell me the story.

"We were on our way to pick you up on orders from DHS. It was right after the initial outbreak happened. Things were still running smoothly, or as smoothly as they possibly could after hundreds of thousands of people began dropping dead and then rising up and attacking the living. They put me in charge of the drop team, gave me a full brief on you and how important you would be to finding out what the fuck had happened. Scott was the actual boots on the ground group commander. The rest of the guys were plain old, no name, spec ops noobs. We had no idea how bad things were about to get, how bad they were out in the demilitarized zones."

I stop her.

"What do you mean? I thought you said that things were going fine."

She nods and takes a long drag on her cigarette and a sip from her can of Bud.

"Yeah, the major cities—New York, Washington, Chicago and L.A., Philly, Cleveland, Pittsburgh, Detroit—were out of the loop. We had already enacted the council of governors, which totally failed. Not because of the zombies or whatever they are, but because the civvies were up in arms and shit about death camps and fucking conspiracy nuts came out of everywhere lead, of course, by Alex Jones and his revivalists. Everyone who wasn't infected went ape shit which, in turn, made it harder to keep quarantine zones locked down. It was a blood bath."

"Jesus," I whisper into my coffee mug and take another drink. "You know he was CIA, right?"

"Who?" she asks, and I say, "Alex Jones."

"No, I didn't. I wonder what they were getting at, then?" she asks.

I shrug my shoulders and shake my head. "Clampdown," I say back to her.

She shrugs her shoulders back and continues. "Anyway, when we got here, the building was already shut down but enough of the infected had breached the city center and were in the building that when we landed on the roof, we—me and Scott—knew that shit was going downhill."

"So, how did you guys get in here?" I ask, pulling out another cigarette and lighting up. This time I take baby hits and manage to get through half of it before wanting to puke.

"I was supposed to stay onboard while Scott and the rest of the spec ops team came down here and grabbed your little tube, but I decided to come along. We were gonna figure out how we were gonna stay behind. When we got here it was overrun already, so we tried to clear out the ones we could and looked around."

The carnage from the lobby made more sense now: the massive amounts of the shell casings, the fact that Carol didn't have much of a face, how the security guards had been overwhelmed.

"When we couldn't find your tube we came back up. Scott and I decided to send the rest of the team up and we would just radio in a fake attack, order them to leave and then we would be officially dead."

"That doesn't explain how you got in here, though. It needs a bioscan or the right key sequence. How did you get past that?" I ask.

"The power went out; the doors swung open enough that Scott could get his hand behind it and pry it open, and when he did we ran inside. The auxiliary power kicked back on a couple of seconds later and the door locked us in here."

I look down at the screens, then over to the three files on the screen to my left. "Dumb luck, that's some shit."

We hear the door to the bathroom open and Skinny Scott comes out; he makes a low whistle and waves his hand in front of his face.

"Don't, seriously, go in there for a good half hour," he says and then flops on the same chair as before, cracks open another beer and begins to stare back out the windows. I look back to the screens and pull the three files into the separate open windows, looking for the earliest date first. I find the cache that I'm looking for and open it up, but wave the screen off.

"Hey, Scott," I say over to him. He lolls his head around to look at me and says, "Wha," which I take as being the same as asking me "What?"

"Put your hand on the wall behind you, you should find a piece that slides up. There's a touch panel under it. When it comes up, tap in one-three-three-one, then turn your chair around. Got it?"

The touchscreen is already lighting up his face halfway through my instructions; he turns his chair around and then the rest of the wall panel slides down to reveal my television screen along with every gaming console that's ever been made. I don't play them, but I used to collect them. It's like comics or baseball cards or CDs or whatever else it is that humans used to collect. And since I had what at one time would have been considered a ton of fucking money, I also have one of the world's last and greatest collections of video games. He slides down to look at all the consoles and games.

"Holy shit," he says as he begins to pull cartridges and CD/DVD cases out of their current alphabetical order.

"Holy shit, you have a mint *Legend of Zelda*, in the fucking box. Kel, he has a mint *Legend of Zelda*." He holds up the dusty gold cardboard box so that Kel can see it.

She looks over at me and I pull out my wireless headphones from my cigarette drawer and toss them to her.

"Here, just put these on if you're gonna play, same code as the panel," I say and Kel hands him the headphones. He looks over to me and holds up another box. I can't see what it is from the desk. I squint but still can't make out the title.

"*Castle*. Fucking. *Vania*. In Japa. Fucking. Nese," he says back to me in complete seriousness and then puts on the headphones and powers up the ancient-looking Nintendo that's halfway through the line up of outdated game systems. At least he has good taste. Kel gives me a weird look. She stands up and walks over to Scott, tapping him on the head.

"Wha?" he says as he hits pause and looks back up to her.

"You're already drunk. Don't stay up late; we should do a security sweep on the building tomorrow. I'm going to lay down," she says and before she turns away he pulls the headphones back up over his ears and salutes her, then loses himself in Simon Belmont's original quest to destroy Dracula. She comes over to me and puts her hand on the desk and leans forward, presumably so that Scott won't hear us, though I doubt she needs to. He's already completely engrossed in the ancient game's pixilated world.

"You know this doesn't make anything better," she says first, then adds, "You're still a monster like Scott said. So don't think that the food or the beer or the games are going to make me, or us, feel different about you in the morning."

I lean back in the chair and light up another cigarette, then pull another set of wireless headphones up from another drawer. The gun is still in the waistline of my pants and she looks nervously from it to my face.

"Kel, I have no idea what happened. Like you said, I was frozen, but I'm about to find out tonight, okay? So don't fucking judge me. You two aren't innocent, either. Let me see if I can guess here: deserters, probably in a relationship, maybe a couple hundred or so murders on your hands from those little covert operations all over the fucking world. Am I right; did I get it?"

She pauses for a few seconds and then says she says, "Yeah, something like that."

I think she's turning around to walk away, but she fakes and returns with a right hook that, as it connects, flips me out of my chair. I rub my jaw and feel my bottom lip getting swollen. I stare down to my hand. There's more of my blood running down my fingers.

"You broke the fucking world, asshole. Do you even get that? The fucking world. And now you're still trying to buy people like you did before everything went to shit because—let me remind you again—of you. Yeah, I've killed some people, and most of them would have shot me if I hadn't shot them first, but you're the monster that did *that*," she says and points out towards the windows.

The fires seem to have intensified. The silence of the night has hidden away the monsters milling about in the street, the wreckage of the cars, and even the broken down facades of the buildings. But the soft orange glowing coming from the horizon line seems as bright as a cluster of supernovas. I stare for a while before she turns away again and moves towards the couch, stretches out on it and closes her eyes.

I look around and find my set of headphones, then get up and sit back down. Scott doesn't even register that there's anything happening outside of the fact that he can't make the last jump on the screen. He's sticking the tip of his tongue out the side of his mouth, sitting cross-legged, and every time he attempts the move, his body jerks up as if it's going to carry the eight-bit hero on the screen forward. I wave my hand over the screen and open the first file again. I bring up the feeds first, then the sites and then the videos.

7.

I leave the video feeds alone; the regular old RSS feeds are easier and lighter on the system, so I dig into those first. The screen pops up with my feed aggregator; there are over 100,000 entries in assorted categories. I do a quick keyword search for words like *beginning, apocalypse, plague, zombie, first stage, infection,* and so on. It cuts the number to just over 60,000.

"Jesus," I whisper. I don't know what I was thinking going straight to the feeds first. When I froze myself there were nearly 300 million blogs available to read. 300 million people who thought that the world really cared about what they thought or what they wrote or what they ate and read and…well, you get it. There were a lot of assholes with nothing better to do.

I start at the very first entry that was in the folder.

June 22nd.

> *Hey everyone, I know I haven't written in a while, but there's been a lot of crazy stuff going on here lately, as I'm sure you all know. The world is steadily getting crazier. Today on CNN there was a whole video on the importance of hygiene in the event of a pandemic, like we're really going to care about washing our hands if there's a global medical emergency.*
>
> *Also, in other news, my band, **Suffering Carpets of the Dawn**, is playing at the Grog Shop on Saturday, yes, this Saturday, so come out and have a great time, hang out and check in with us after the show for a free badge to unlock a new set of credits for our album. See ya there!*

Okay, so it's not a promising start. I do another search, this time I do a random search for thee words: *outbreak*, *government* and *hysteria*.

August 12th

> *Holy Shit, it is going down. I can't leave the house because there's a curfew so I'm updating the old blog. Yesterday I was walking to the store on the corner and I saw three huge armored vehicles roll down the street. They stopped at the intersection and let three dozen or so soldiers out and then they started setting up four-way stops and checkpoints. Fucking weekend warriors were going crazy, telling people to go home and that there was now a curfew and that food rations would be handed out door to door. It's happening man; they're using this fucking outbreak or whatever it is to start their global agenda man, Alex is right, we gotta rise up and take it back. Just Listen to his special report on Prison Planet.com…*

There's more but I stop reading. I put my head down into my hands and sigh. Jesus, I can't believe that people were this fucking stupid. I know if I keep reading I'm going to start to think that, if it was or is my fault, I may have done the world a huge fucking favor.

I look over to where Scott is sitting, still playing *Castlevania*. He's pumping the buttons with thumbs that could probably play the game on autopilot. The glow from the screen makes his face look ashen. Shadows and muted colors dance a graceful ballet on the walls and windows of the office. He pauses the game long enough to light another cigarette and take a gulp from his beer. I light up another one of my own and decide to put the feeds away and move to the videos. Fuck accuracy of information, I can't handle this shit.

The first video is footage from a news chopper outside of a shopping mall. It looks completely normal. I pull my headphones on and listen to the audio report from the reporter in the chopper. It's entitled "Garrettsville Mall Massacre."

> *"There's been an outbreak of what health authorities are calling the H6N7 strain of flu, at the Garrettsville Mall. Police and security from the mall are on the scene and are attempting to lock down the mall and establish a quarantine zone. Be advised that if you are watching this and know someone in the mall or are someone currently trapped in the mall, that there is a standing order by officials to use lethal force on anyone coming out of, or going into the mall at the present time. Authorities on the ground are advising that you please stay put or away from the scene."*

As the reporter continues and the chopper lowers itself down to get a better shot, police cruisers and tactical vans begin establishing a perimeter around the complex. The cops jump out of their vehicles and look like black knights defending a pointless citadel. Their full head-to-toe riot gear glistens in the sun and instead of normal insignias and badges they have the big white DHS emblazoned on their backs. They're all carrying heavy munitions, lots of firepower, military spec stuff you wouldn't imagine cops having.

The camera on the chopper zooms in on a couple who have made their way out of one of the bigger department stores. They're running towards a group of police who look like they're motioning for the two to stop. They keep coming; the woman has blood running down the front of her shirt and is holding her hand up to her neck. The man is almost dragging her along behind him. Poor fuckers don't even know what's going on. Behind them another group of people has made it out. The police put their hands up and then raise their weapons, sight down the couple and, when they don't stop, they begin shooting.

Blood and tissue and most likely fragments of bone fly from the first couple. Their clothes begin to turn from brightly advertised consumer goods to a comically bright red and then to crimson-soaked rags. A couple of the cops land head shots on the woman and her face splits into three separate parts. Pink and grey chunks of brain blow backwards, up into the air and then come to settle on separate sides of the bodies.

The second group of escapees hit the ground but meets a similar end; then more and more people begin to run out of the mall, filtering out in clusters of threes and fours. Hundreds of people are gunned down in the same fashion as the first couple. The feed from the chopper cuts to two newsanchors in a green room studio. One is a man in a black suit and impeccably crisp, white shirt, which is offset by the purple bags under his eyes. The second is a bleach blonde woman who looks like she's about twenty-five and hasn't eaten in months. The man looks down at the screen that's embedded into the large desk in front of him. He starts to turn green. The woman has her hand up to her open mouth.

The video goes on for a few more seconds; the man attempts to read the script, but after a few brief sentences about how the station should have warned viewers about the shocking content, he turns his head away and sprays sick behind him. The woman begins crying. The video stops. The video aggregator pulls down another clip.

It's an on the ground, hand cam, gorilla-style piece of footage entitled "My Hood." It looks like it was taken with a tablet or a phone. The audio sucks, so it was probably a device not running my app. The voice sounds like a teenage boy; I'd say he sounds fifteen, tops. His face comes into frame a few seconds later. It's a bad close up and even with the terrible resolution from the device's camera you can see he has a terrible haircut that makes him look like he's a girl. He's got a pretty horrific case of acne and braces fighting an overbite of epic proportions that make his words almost unintelligible.

"So, yeah, I woke up today. Which is cool, I guess. I haven't heard from Mom or Dad yet, but they were downtown, and that was locked down about three days ago, so they haven't been able to leave their buildings yet. I got an email from Mandy this

morning; she said that her college was about the same, but she was safe. I have enough food for now, though I blew through all the Mountain Dew last night. The television doesn't have anything on it anymore except emergency broadcasts, which blows. But the real reason I'm taking this video is 'cause after I woke up I looked out the window and there was this outside…"

He turns the device around in his hand and sticks it through the curtains. As the camera spins, it tries to focus on everything, making my eyes want to cross. Shitty device doesn't even have steady hand technology; he should have been running the app. Then as the outside comes into focus, you can tell that the sky is bright and clear, the clouds are heavy and white. It's a picturesque suburb where every house is some slight variation of the next one. But as he pans the device from left to right you begin to see lumbering silhouettes making their way up and down the sidewalks and street. They look like the broken, crooked bodies that I saw out of the window, like the crooked man when I first woke up: empty, open eyes, grey-green skin, some have dried blood stains on their clothes, and some look impeccable except for their skin.

They stalk silently, panning their heads from left to right, looking aimlessly at everything, as if it didn't register that they were outside or that they were looking at the ground or sky or plants. One of the figures that passes by is a woman in a nightgown, flowing white and tattered, nearly sheer, showing off everything. Her belly looks distended but then I realize that she is, or in this case, *was*, pregnant. Her hair is a tangled mess of auburn and crusty, dried chunks. She's the closest of the monsters to the house that the kid is in. She slowly turns her head from side to side, as if it were nearly impossible for her to move her neck.

She takes a step forward, then, as if she knows the kid is in the house, as if she sees the device he's holding or maybe even his hand, she begins to turn. She begins to walk toward the camera. One foot in front of the other, she silently hobbles over the grass towards the house. Her mouth agape, her teeth look as if she's been eating black liquorice, her tongue is swollen and green. Her nightgown moves on the wind and if it wasn't for the way that she's stumbling around like she's just woke up from a three-day bender, she would look like she's floating. She continues forward.

I know what's going to happen here; the kid doesn't. It's in every cliché monster movie I've ever seen. It's the truth. The camera pulls back around; the kid pulls it back to his face and starts talking again.

"I don't know what's going on..." he begins, and then there's the crashing of glass. And then the device is dropped. He runs out to see what it was, then a scream, a gut-wrenching, horrible scream. A scream of innocence and first and second and third kisses not kissed and fucks not fucked and beers not drank; pain and terror bleed out of the audio and into my ears, the noise makes my stomach drop. I want to reach out and tell him he's a cliché. But I can't because he's not, this is how it happened. I'm watching it, living it with him. This is the legacy of the internet. This is shooting the pain; this is collecting communal scars on the fabric of society and all I can think about, the only thought that's running through my head, is that he should have had a better device. Something that would have allowed him to see what was happening without taking his eyes off a screen.

The clip keeps going; the audio catches every plea and cry. Every tear drop, every single sound of pain and all I can do is watch as his bloody and mangled body hits the floor like a five pound sack of potatoes.

I stop the video, pull the frame out of the aggregator and drag it towards the recycle bin. But I stop my finger before I can throw it away and look over to Scott. He's passed out on the floor, the screen is still running and the game is still going. He must be lying on the controller because Simon Belmont is jumping up and down in the same corner of Dracula's castle. Over and over again, eight-bit Simon tries to get up and jump from landing to landing and each time he falls.

THIS IS THE END

Scott's Labatt Blue pint is lying on its side, empty, next to an ashtray full of cigarette butts and I'm about to throw this kid's life away.

"What the fuck is wrong with me?" I say.

I leave the "My Hood" video up on my desktop but minimize it. I turn and watch the glow of the fires come from the horizon, creeping closer and closer to the city center. Running fire, wild fire coming to cleanse and I want to cry. But it isn't for the city, or Skinny Scott, or Simon Belmont unable to jump and slay his demon. It's not for the kid on the video, not for my dad or Janet or Phil. I want to cry because I'm watching the last seconds of this kid's life and all I care about is screen resolution, megapixel quality, device stability and processing speed.

I watch more videos, more scenes like the mall, more eulogies and last wills and testaments, more *I love yous* and *I miss yous* and *Please, God, help mes*. Official reports and news footage full of more lies and more carnage and more of the press' feeble attempt to pacify regular people too scared out of their minds to heed official positions of power.

I even watch as the President of the United States tells everyone that things will be better. I watch as a grown man lies to millions of people as if they are children, children that know better, but that can't do a damn thing about it except get spanked for doing the right thing. Then I get to the last few folders of videos that have anything to do with all the keywords.

I lean back in my chair and light a cigarette. It's nearly morning and I decide to make another pot of coffee. I stare at the morning sun, cresting the sprawling dead remains, muting the fires just for a second or two with its natural brilliance.

I still want to cry but I can't.

I sit there and watch as the last bit of pure, unfiltered sunshine shimmers against the steel and glass and still-brown surface of Lake Erie. After it's made its way past the horizon line, I can't see it anymore, engulfed by the rising black and grey smoke of the now not so distant fires; it looks cancerous and wicked, like the eye of God passing judgment. I turn around and continue to work my way through all the files. I don't stop until I pass out.

* * *

I'm dreaming again, but this time it's not the same dream I always have. I try and make sure that I know this is a dream. I try and tell myself to remember that I didn't have the crowd dream. To remember that I had a dream of pure white silence, blinding perfection and glistening raw nothing. But it's a dream and I'm sidetracked by the fact that there is nothing. Like I'm back in the freeze chamber, like I'm dead again, my mind is racing but my heartbeat and breathing feels calm. I see the world come into focus and it looks like a stream of codes. Big codes, small codes, little pieces of code are everywhere, they make up everything. I can manipulate the code; I can pull the sections and strains out into the air and make flowers or park benches, trees or a car. Everything is unified and mathematical and I can make it into whatever I want.

I stand in the bleach bottle white space and tap and pull at the codes, but now I'm not just building, but rebuilding the world. Rebuilding the city, rebuilding the sidewalks and street lights. I make sound and it sounds like Ping. *The sound comes and goes every other minute.* Ping. Ping. Ping Ping Ping Ping Ping Ping.

The more I put things back together the more clear and definite the sound becomes, like it's right next to my ears, like it's in my head. It starts out as a soft and subtle undertone, just under the surface of the great nothing; then as I move faster and faster and faster it becomes louder and louder and louder until I can't stand it anymore. Until I wake up.

Kel and Scott are standing in front of the desk and looking at me as I raise my head up. A thick strand of drool that smells horrible follows my bottom lip.

"What?" I say at them.

Kel points to my desktop, the screens are still going, and her eyes look like bright white tea saucers.

"Are you messaging with someone?" she asks.

"What?" I say back and then realize that, as we are talking I hear the *Ping* sound that was in my dream. I tap the screen and bring it out of hibernation. I stop and look down. I have eight unread messages, sent today, all within the last hour or so.

8.

"That's impossible. I thought you said that there wasn't an internet anymore," I say to Scott. He's standing at a slight angle next to Kel and he looks as if he's going to heave all over everything. Beads of sweat glisten on his forehead and the hair around his temples is soaked.

"There isn't supposed to be any," he says, then puts his hand up to his mouth as if he's keeping the whole of his insides from coming out of his mouth.

"Go to the bathroom, Scott," says Kel and he moves past her and then the desk; I can hear his stomach making horrible noises as he runs into the bathroom.

"And turn on the water in the sink, for Christ's sake; no one wants to hear that," I say to him through the door. Kel is already next to me behind the desk, looking over my shoulder at the screens.

"This is one of CENTCOM's handles. It's trying to ping in," she says. She smells earthy and unwashed, though that could just be her clothing. She nudges me out of the way so that she can see more of the screen; I protest and then get up and motion for her to sit down.

"This could just be the main servers trying to establish any sort of satellite connection, but it could also be someone on the other end," she says. She opens up a command prompt, copies the messages and starts typing in directives I've never seen. Her fingers tap at the screen as if they are on autopilot, her slender hands moving at speeds that I've only seen on a couple of other coders outside of myself. She's good.

"What did you say you did in the military, again?" I ask her while I stare at the efficiency of her keystrokes. The complexity of the commands she's laying out is staggering and if things were different—if I wasn't so absolutely sure that she hates my very existence and the world hadn't ended—I would probably ask her out on a date.

"I never said, but I was in a spec ops intelligence unit—encryption, data forensics—but I've been working with computers my whole life. I modded your app shortly after it came out," she says without looking up from the screen. The glow of the monitors mixed with the morning haze gives her face an attractive quality that I didn't see before.

"It's definitely not just remote access for emergencies; someone saw you ping in and is trying to communicate. Though, again, it could just be a prerecorded message." She finishes typing the last bit of commands and then the monitor to our left loads a fresh vid-feed.

The seal of the United States pops up, the words "Department of Homeland Security" encircle it over and over again, in the background there's a giant flowing American flag.

"Rob. Motherfucker, he was watching everything the whole time," I say in a whisper and she looks up at me and asks, "What?"

"Robert McMillan. He came to visit me the day before I was frozen; he was in my office without me knowing, just showed up with some juiced-up knuckle draggers when I was in the bathroom."

"You personally knew Robert McMillan? Jesus, you are evil," she says back to me. I look down and stare as if I'm going to say something, but I don't and just nod my head in agreement.

"Anyway, I can play the video if you want," she says.

I look at the spinning letters surrounding the seal. "Did you make sure that this wasn't some kind of hidden thing, waiting to come up and seize control of the servers?" I ask back and she nods her head.

"I've singled it out from the other messages. It definitely originated outside of the main servers; it's not even on the ghost drives. This was sent to here from a remote location." She gets up out of the chair and motions for me to sit. The faucet in the bathroom is still running and we both cringe at the horrific heaving sounds coming from behind the closed door.

"You think we should wait for Scott?" I ask her and she shrugs her shoulders and says, "We can replay it for him if he really wants to see it, but I doubt he's coming out of there anytime soon."

I nod and then move my hand towards the screen but hesitate before I tap play.

I start to say, "What if this crashes the—" but Kel moves over the desk to tap the screen but stops after her chest brushes against my hand.

She quickly stands up and says, "It's not going to. I've isolated it. Worst that can happen is that this unit and whatever it's tied to goes down. Which one are the lights and locks on?"

I point to the far right screen. She crosses her arms and looks at me like I'm several types of stupid and says, "There, now press play, please."

I move towards the screen. It's the simplest movement to tap a screen, that's why everything went to touch-sensitive displays. I don't want to touch anything, but I do. The background music sounds news-like and patriotic. The face of Robert McMillan comes to life in front of us on the screen. He's standing at a podium with a yellowed-looking picture of the Capital Building behind him. He's smiling and staring into the camera as if he—then it hits me. I stop the video.

"What the hell did you do that for?" Kel asks me. I put my head down and it's almost too much to say. I can feel it deep inside my chest, the unfamiliar feeling of amusement. The sheer joy and absurdity of the thought process, but also at the fact that I think I just figured everything out. I feel the sound before I hear it. I'm laughing. I'm almost near the point of uncontrollable hiccupping, gagging, and tear-filled laughter.

"I'm not a monster," I say to her and she slides one foot back, which, I guess if I were in her shoes, I would, too. I do probably look like I've just lost it. Maybe I have. The very idea, the very thought that I just had, though it makes sense, sounds completely crazy.

"What?" she asks and I try to say what I'm thinking but I can't. I just can't stop laughing.

"Motherfucker," I get out before I topple over in my chair and hit the floor, a move that makes me laugh at myself and keep laughing until I feel the little tears forming behind my closed eyes.

"Have you lost your mind?" asks Kel. She's taken a couple of steps back towards the couch, back towards where their guns are. I wave my hand and try to say, "Yes," but I can't, so I nod my head and say, "Don't," instead. I'm laughing so hard that I begin coughing and then that turns into me gasping for air on the floor. I'm lying on my back staring into my ceiling, staring at all the exposed duct work that's beginning to turn yellow from smoke and dust. Skinny Scott is still in the bathroom, the water has stopped and he's moved on to making groans and grunts.

I look over at the door and then back up to the ceiling. "I've been there before, brother," I say to myself.

Kel asks, "What?" again and I just shake my head and say, "It's nothing."

She moves a little closer and then says, "No, I was wondering what was so funny?"

"Oh, that. Yeah," I say and start giggling again. Kel frowns and comes over to me and holds out her hand. I take it and she pulls me up. I brush dust off my suit and look her square in the eyes.

"I'm not the monster," I say with a smile. She still looks as if she fell off a truck headed to an Indigo Girl's reunion concert but some of the hardness has gone from her features; her eyes are a deep green-grey and her skin is pale but smooth. She looks unimpressed with my statement.

"How do you mean?" she asks.

I point to the screen where Robert McMillan, former Head and Secretary of The Department of Homeland Security is paused with a million dollar, shit-eating grin on his face, and say, "He's the fucking monster; he did it."

Scott comes out of the bathroom with a washcloth draped around his neck and looking more pale than green.

"What did I miss?" He asks.

* * *

"Let me say this out loud so I can get it straight in my head," says Scott and then he continues, "You're telling us that Robert McMillan launched some kind of biological attack on the United States, just so he could become President?"

"Yes," I say. They're both sitting on the couch and I'm in front of the television screen with the credits to *Castlevania* running on replay.

"Rob is—was—whatever—a completely power obsessed freak. The guy already, literally, thought that he ran the fucking government, which, for the most part, he did. But still, even with that, it was never the king's seat."

Kel is looking at me like I'm all sorts of stupid, again, and Scott is vacillating between watching me and the screen. I don't know how many more times I can really go through the explanation.

"Okay, one more time with feeling," I say and then start all over again. "Robert-fucking-evil-McMillan, through the Department of Homeland Security, launched an attack. Whether it was intentionally going to be large or not is unknown at this point, but that's why I need you," I point to Kel and then continue. "He launched a biological attack so that he could use that to gain enough power to crown himself President. Or dictator. Or whatever."

I keep pacing back and forth in front of the screen and waving my hands. I feel like a college professor on speed; I can't get the thoughts out quick enough.

"He put everything together. He had Phil, my layer—remember the one who apparently ran off with my ex wife?" They nod and I continue on. "He had Phil get me all doped up and drunk the night before I was frozen so that I couldn't change my mind—not that I was going to, but still. Rob was pissed when I came out about some of the secret shit we were doing at that press conference. Pissed enough to visit me the next day and threaten me to my face. He knows that I keep everything backed up in triplicate; he also knew that if I decided to, I could drop a big fucking neutron bomb of truth about what the Department was up to. He fucking killed the world and it back fired, but he doesn't—or didn't—care about that. He got what he wanted, and blamed me. That's why you guys were sent here. Not to pick me up; you were supposed to kill me."

"That doesn't really take the pressure off of you; you still helped him do this," says Kel. She looks like she believes some of it. I can't stop thinking about her at the screens tapping away; her bumping her breasts on my hand was a bonus. I haven't been with a woman in roughly a year and a half. So pretty much any contact with a member of the opposite sex will have that effect on me right now, but there's something about Kel.

She catches me looking at her funny and asks, "Well?"

"Well, what?" I say back and Scott repeats what she said.

"She said it doesn't take the blame off of you, dude." He looks better; we made some biscuits and chicken before we sat down. At least he doesn't look like he's dying anymore, though the rings underneath his bloodshot eyes tell a different story

"It does," I say and stop pacing. "I had no idea what the fuck he and Phil were up to. I knew a couple things, easy things like railguns and high-tech camouflage shit; Phil told me about Project Mobile the night before I was frozen. I guess he figured that it wouldn't matter, but I didn't know about any of the real deals. I knew we had a chemical and neurological development team," I say but Kel interrupts me.

"So you did know," she says folding her arms and looking away, out the window again, as if she needs to hold onto the fact that I'm still the real monster.

I put my hand up to my face and then move it up and rub my bald head. "Jesus, are you even listening to me?" I said.

Scott stops me this time. "Dude, seriously, it's the same thing. You might not have known exactly what you were working on, but you knew something, right?"

I open my mouth to rebut him, but I can't, so I close it and look at both of them. They still hate me. They still think that I am responsible for all of this. I look out towards the windows. The smoke from the fires meanders from the horizon line and into the sky like huge lumbering caterpillars.

"Kel, do you think you could comb over my servers?" She looks back to me again, but this time a little of that hate is replaced by a twinkle.

"Too easy," she says.

"Okay, good. Here," I say and move over towards my desk, motioning for her to follow me. I sit down, power everything up and put in all of my passwords.

Everything comes to life in under a second. The screens dim for a half a second and we both notice it.

"What was that?" she asks. I get up and motion for her to sit again.

"I just opened up everything in the building except the door controls for you to look over. There's a couple of hundred server racks that are powered up right now, waiting for you to get cracking; it's a pretty big power drain."

Her jaw opens slightly, there's a small trace smile in her lips, but she quickly tries to hide her enthusiasm.

"What am I looking for exactly?" she asks.

I point at the screen that Robert McMillan's face is on.

"Anything to do with that fucker, and what happened."

"Awesome. I'm gonna lay down then if you two are gonna geek out," says Scott. He spreads out on the couch and puts his feet up on one of the arm rests. I walk over and knock his boots off; he gets up too fast for his own good. He sits back down and holds his stomach for a few seconds as if he's going to puke again.

"Nope. We, my good man, are going to see about my car," I say.

"You have a car?" asks Scott. He's still deciding whether or not getting up is a good idea.

"Yep, a Ford Focus."

"Dude, you were like the richest guy in the world before all this shit and you have a Ford Focus?" he asks.

"You've never seen my Ford Focus," I say and walk towards the door.

9.

When the doors open up I instantly stop; the smell of rotten and decaying flesh is too much. Scott must not have been paying any attention because he runs right into my back. I put my hand up and he does the same. I had forgotten what was out here. Scott can't hold back and heaves behind me. I jump forward and step on someone's hand; the sound of bones cracking under the heel of my shoe is almost enough to make me lose it. I suck in a mouthful of air and hold my breath. Jesus, even the air has the same sickening smell to it.

I turn around and Scott looks like hell again, he's turning from pale back to a sickly shade of green and I watch as he fights another urge to spew. He looks over at me and I motion for him to follow. We make it to the other side of the security door; he clicks on the flashlight and we both sit down on the top step. I take my pack of smokes out and light one up, then hand it over for him to take. He shakes his head.

"No, I'm good. I just need to breathe," he says.

I suck back and watch the cherry light up then get up. "You good?"

He waits a few more seconds and then replies, "Yeah, just wasn't…I just forgot."

I nod and say, "Me too." And then start back down the steps towards the ground floor and the garage.

I don't even know if the car is still there or not. Really, I just wanted to clear my head. I'm almost a hundred percent sure my theory on Rob is right, but even if I'm wrong, he still has to have more to do with this than most people thought.

We move forward; we keep on going through the motions of stepping over each other in silence. Scott is in front now, then I'll round out and beat him forward on a landing and he'll hand the flashlight off to me for a while.

It's only six floors until we hit the garage then we'll have to figure a way to get from the doorway to where my car is parked.

If I'm right, then there won't be a large chance of running into anything like the crooked man down in the garage. Even when everything was normal, I only staffed two security guys down here at all times.

Let's face it, if anyone had gotten into the garage, they could have easily blown the building. There wasn't much that I was going to be able too do about that. We move in silence the entire way until we see the big capital G on the wall.

"This it?" asks Scott.

I nod back and say, "Yeah," while I'm putting my face to the window in the door. I tip-toe up and look around but it's no use; it's pitch black in there.

"Fuck," I whisper and slide back down onto the souls of my shoes. Scott looks terrible; I should have just done this on my own. He's leaning hard on the wall like a drunk trying to piss a straight line. Every other breath he takes is strained and the arm that's extended out and propping him up is visibly shaking. "You sure you're all right?" I ask him and he looks over at me and nods his head and then tries to make it look like *fuck-all* didn't run over his body this morning.

After a minute or two of standing upright and trying to fake it, he leans back on the wall, exhales and says, "No."

"Drink too much?" I ask back, though I already know the answer. He stands up straight again and surprises me by shaking his head back and forth slowly.

"Then what is it?" I ask him again. This time I'm holding the flashlight and looking for the little fingerprint reader that should still have power.

"Last time I had to fight those things was the raid on this building, time before that was down in Nashville. Both were just as bad."

"Oh, Jesus, Scott. Don't tell me you have PTSD or some other bullshit excuse that'll make you freeze up like a—"

I barely have time to get the "a" out before he slams me into the wall next to the door. He's breathing heavily and spit is pooling on his lip. I see the face of pure, unadulterated, scary, physical strength for the first time in my life. I'm not going to lie; if I could have, I would have pissed my pants.

"No, I don't, dude, and if you say one more thing like that, one more fucking snide remark, I will carve out your kneecaps, drag you outside and laugh as you scream your lungs out while those things eat you alive. Got it?"

I nod my head yes and feel pain shooting down my spine. I can barely breathe; his hand is wrapped up in my dress shirt and he's pulled it tight against my throat. I can feel my face turning redder and redder on its way to blue. After a few more tense seconds and a stare that I'm pretty sure would make Satan himself think twice, he lets me go.

I begin to apologize, "Sorry, I just—"

But he stops me and then starts brushing me off. "No, it's cool. I lost it for a second. My bad," he says.

I make a mental note that Scott is officially off my list of people to fuck with and then turn back to look for the sensor. I look up to the ceiling for the reflection of the red laser beam then shine the flashlight over and see the black pad sticking out of the wall. I turn back and shine the light on Skinny Scott and he looks like he's gonna be sick again.

"I found it. How do you want to do this?" I ask him.

He looks at me and shrugs. "I'll take point, I guess."

I look back at him and he says, "It means I'll go first."

I nod and pull out the pistol from the waist of my pants and flick the safety off, hand him the flash light and then I move back towards the fingerprint scanner. I hear the beep and the magnetic locks release with a stomach-turning click. Scott grabs the handle, pulls the flashlight up, clicks it on and pulls the door open wide. I run behind him and grab hold of his shirt and we move into the garage.

The beam from the flashlight cuts through the darkness in the garage as he sweeps it from left to right. There are still four rows of cars parked in the garage which means that it's almost full. I'm still holding onto his shirt and he looks back at me. I let go but stay directly behind him. He looks back out towards where the cone of the flashlight ends on the far wall of the garage. He signals for me to be quiet, and I nod back to him.

"Which way?" he asks in a tone barely above a whisper.

"Towards the left, that's where my spot is," I say back.

He moves slowly and I follow his every footstep. He shines the light forward and we make it to the first set of parked cars. He crouches down next to a midsized sedan and I follow him and crouch next to him. He chokes up on the flashlight and covers the beam with his hand. He turns to me and motions for me to be quiet, then he flicks off the light and we sit in the darkness. The car has what feels like an eighth of an inch-thick layer of dust on it, and I reflexively cringe at having to put my suit jacket up to it.

We lean on the car and wait for, I presume, the sound of anything but us moving. I can feel my nose and chest start to tighten up from the dust and I begin to wiggle my nose. After a few seconds I yank on his shirt and he clicks the light back on and puts it under his face.

"What?" he whispers back.

"If there was anything in here, don't you think that they would have seen the big fucking ray of light from the flashlight?" I ask him.

He looks around and then says, "Good point."

We stand up cautiously and scan the perimeter again. Nothing moves.

"Ok, where's your spot again?" he asks and I look around but can't see a thing.

"Give me the light?" I ask. He looks down at it and then reluctantly hands it over. I scan towards where I think the car should be and then I see it. It's still there, in all its non-elegant glory and complete ugliness.

"That's it," I say and then I take off without giving back the light to him.

He tries to protest for a second but then gives up and follows. I stop at the hood of my mighty metal rhino. Seeing it makes me want to cry. Not because I missed it, though I know when I get into it, I will have. But just the sight of something that's mine and that hasn't changed is enough to make me want to get emotional.

"I seriously can't believe you drive a Ford Focus," he says back to me. He starts to walk around the car and look at it, inspecting the tires and the body.

"This car has more technology and safety features than most tanks," I say back to him. I'm walking around the opposite side and running my hand over the hood. Even with all the dust and moisture on it, it still looks beautiful.

"Think of it this way," I say back as I fumble in my suit pocket for the keyless ignition. "This thing is like my office upstairs. It's got solar cell membranes, bulletproof glass, composite Kevlar carbon fiber reinforced frame and run-flats, a fully functioning real-time sync to the units upstairs and drink holders."

"Yeah, no, that sounds awesome," he says back to me, "but why a Focus?"

"Would you expect one of the world's richest men to drive around in a Ford Focus?"

He thinks about it for a few seconds and then looks back to me. "Another good point."

I hand him back the flashlight and push the unlock button on the key fob and watch as the latches rise up along the four doors. Scott stops for a second and looks behind him. I'm too busy getting into the car to really notice what he's doing.

I sit down in the seat and run my hands along the dashboard controls and dials. "I missed you," I say to the car, and I can almost hear it saying, *I missed you too, Jeff.*

I click on the dome light and close my eyes for a second at how bright everything is. I look over to where Scott is still standing next to the right headlight. He's scanning back and forth and looks like he's focused on something in the garage. I open the driver's side door and stand up. "Hey, what is it?" I ask.

He shushes me and moves his hand like he's telling a crowd to quiet down. I stop and listen. Then from the right, we hear something that isn't us. Scott jumps and spins the light around to where he thinks the noise is coming from.

For a few heartbeats there is silence again. I double-check the safety on my gun and strain my eyes to see if I can make anything out in the dark. The noise repeats again, but this time it seems closer. He moves back to the passenger door and then opens it out and stands behind it.

"Hey, you got power?" he asks and I say, "Yeah,"

"Then turn on the headlights."

I sit back down in the seat and look at the dial that controls the headlights; I look back out into the darkness. I hesitate for a few seconds and then decide to say fuck it, and turn them on full-blast. The headlights seem to illuminate the whole garage and instantly make everything cast deep and dark shadows on the wall.

We both hear the sound again. This time it's coming from the left hand side of the car, the one closest to me. I pull the door closed.

Scott turns out the flashlight and stoops down to look inside at me and then says, "Brights."

I give him a look that says "Really?" and he nods twice. I click on the brights and the whole garage comes into tight focus. Then we see the first one, then the second and then the third and then so on and so forth until I count about twelve. Scott gets into the car and closes the door.

"Turn the lights off, please," he says without looking at me. I click everything off and the garage is solid black again. I hear someone say, "Fuck," but to tell you the truth, I can't remember which one of us said it first.

* * *

"You're sure this thing is safe?" he asks.

"Yeah," I whisper then add, "What the fuck are we gonna do?"

"I have no idea. This was your plan," he says back.

I didn't think that there would be twelve of them. If nothing else, I thought maybe one—two tops. But twelve? I never thought there would be twelve.

We hear the first of the monsters' fists hit one of the windows and it makes me jump; I couldn't tell about Scott, but I'm pretty sure he did the same. It sounds like it was right outside my window. It was a dull thud at first, as if it were just trying to spook us out. Then, as the others make their way over, they start to pound on the car; the thudding, open palm slaps begin to become fist slams.

They start at the hood and then work their way up to the windows and back around to the hatchback.

Twelve sets of hands start bashing into everything and everywhere all at once. The car isn't easy to rock, it weighs too much, and from what I have seen of these things, which is admittedly very little, I don't think they have the strength to tip it. But the continual beating the body and doors and windows are taking is enough to make me think that this might not be the safest place for us to be.

"I could gun it?" I ask him.

"What?" he says back, and though I can't really make out the expression on his face, I'm pretty sure he thinks I'm fucking nuts.

"I could start her up and try and get them off of us," I explain.

"Where are you gonna go?" he asks back and then adds, "I don't know if you saw or not, but it's not like there aren't any other cars in the garage."

"What the fuck else are we gonna do, sit in here and wait 'em out? They already know we're here—might as well try and move ourselves closer to the door."

He begins to object but as he starts to tell me how stupid the idea is, one of them slams their face into his window.

"Fuck! JUST DO IT," he yells and grabs hold of the dashboard.

I push the power button and the engine roars to life; the headlights cut back through the murky darkness and reveal the multitude of bloody fist and palm prints that are scattered over the windows. I shove the automatic gear shift into drive and floor it. The monster directly in front of the car goes down and we bounce over it like a pothole as we move forward, towards the first row of cars.

The other monsters try and hold onto the car as it rams its way forward. Their hands streak across the windows and leave smears of sticky black fluid and blood in their wake.

"TURN THE FUCKING WHEEL," I hear him scream as he reaches over to grab the wheel.

I slam the steering wheel all the way to the left and we narrowly miss the row of cars directly in front of us. I try to slam on the brakes or make another turn but can't. We smash into the roll down doors of the garage. The airbags deploy and instantly Scott and I are thrown into the backs of our seats.

"Oh, shit, that sucked," he says as he tries to push the airbag out of his way.

I move my own airbag out of the way and say, "Not as bad as that." The door to the garage is off its track and I can see dull yellow daylight leaking around the perimeter of the door.

Scott looks to the door and says, "Fuck."

The monsters catch up to us and start beating at the windows again, this time with even more resolve to get at the two of us. One of them is standing next to my window and I can make out the familiar face of an intern that must have gotten trapped here.

His face is sagging and discolored but virtually unscathed, however from the neck down he's covered in the same sticky black goo and dried blood as all the others. His once white shirt is dingy and discolored. His hands are mashed flesh sticks; his hands are nothing more than bloody stumps from smashing at the window.

"I liked this better before we could see them," I say over to Scott.

"I liked this better when we were upstairs," he says back.

I put the car into reverse and slam back down on the gas. Another of the monsters falls prey to my mighty Ford. This time I can actually control the car, and after I feel the thing's body dislodge from underneath, I slam on the breaks and put us back into drive.

We make it around the next row of cars, but the monsters have a target now and follow us. I stop and throw us into reverse again.

"What the fuck are you doing? We're almost to the door," says Scott. I look over to him and put my arm behind his headrest.

I look back towards the group and smile. "Thinning out the herd," I reply as I slam on the gas and smash into the monsters, sending yet another one underneath the car and two more bouncing off the back and into the air.

I spin the wheel and pull us back behind the original row of cars and roll back over one of the bodies on the floor of the garage. As the tire bounces over what must have been its head, we hear a sickening pop followed by a crunch. A thick strand of blood shoots out from underneath the front driver's side wheel. Scott pulls his hand up to his mouth and I choke back the breakfast that's becoming lodged in my throat.

The other monsters don't seem to care about their fallen and run headlong into the hood of the Focus as I put it back into drive and surge the car forward again.

"Seriously, are they that stupid?" I say, and Scott grabs hold of the dashboard again.

"Yeah, they just keep coming—trick is to take headshots, or at least destroy the brain."

There are what appear to be eight still moving, with one on the ground trying to crawl towards the back of the car as I pull the hood towards the door to the stairs.

"Time to shoot," says Scott as he throws open his door. I shut down the car and do the same.

"Remember, aim for their heads," he says back to me as he's sighting down the one closest to us. I see him inhale, hold his breath and then squeeze the trigger. The sound from his gun is massive in the open space of the garage. The bullet slams into the head of his target and explodes shell fragments, bone and brain backwards. The monster goes down in seconds.

I pull my pistol out, sight down the next one and pull the trigger. The shot lands low, ripping open the thing's abdomen and allowing more black liquid and blood to spill out onto the garage floor. It staggers backwards for a few seconds, then rights itself and continues forward. I adjust my aim and pull the trigger again, this time the bullet hits the middle of its face and sends large pieces of eye and jawbone out behind it. It goes down like the other a few seconds later.

Scott takes down two more with controlled shots. Each one a perfect headshot, each neat entry wound accompanied by an equally messy explosion of brain and blood and tissue. He moves towards the hatchback of the Focus and I follow. The next one I aim for is hopelessly crooked, like the first one that I encountered in the lobby of my office. He's wearing torn black jeans and a tattered T-shirt that has the name of some obscure band on it. I hold my breath, pull the trigger and watch him fall. I hear Scott scream and I look over before I have the chance to congratulate myself on the kill. His neck is stretched tight and veins are protruding; his face is red and he begins to fire wildly at the last three.

"Come on, fuckers! COME ON! COME GET SOME," he yells and moves towards the shambling husks.

I try to follow behind him and shoot but I can't get a clear shot off without actually aiming at him. His shots hit bone and body and arms and legs. The monsters go down but they quickly resume their pursuit. The gun in his hand clicks empty and he keeps pulling the trigger. Tears are streaming down his face and he's still walking towards the three bloodied and tattered remains on two legs.

He reaches the first and lands a square punch to its face, sending his fist smashing through its flesh and skull. The monster goes down and I take a step back at his absolute lack of control. I've never seen anyone actually punch through someone's face before, but I blink away the surprise as another monster comes into my peripheral vision. I spin and pull the gun up and squeeze the trigger, the muzzle is point-blank with the monster's forehead and, after the noise, the top of its head becomes nonexistent.

Scott pulls his hand out of the hole and flicks carnage onto the ground. He lines up with the next one but I push him out of the way and to the ground before he has time to swing again. I shove the barrel of the gun into the last one's eye and pull the trigger, sending it flying back a good two feet. It folds onto itself and doesn't move.

He gets up, flashes me a look that makes me want to pee my pants and runs over to the one that's still crawling on the ground.

It's one of the monsters I hit with the car and its legs took the brunt of the assault. It reaches up towards him and he slaps its hand away and begins to stomp its skull with his boots. A few seconds later its head splits open like a ripe melon. Scott doesn't notice and continues on. Tears stream down his face; his breathing is labored and frantic. He's muttering a mixture of curses and grunts with every stomp; he doesn't stop until he slips in the gore and slams into the concrete floor.

He lays there on the garage floor, amid the gore and pieces of bone and flesh, the car's bloody tire tracks and the dirt. He closes his eyes and starts laughing. I walk over and nudge him with the tip of my shoe and he opens his eyes again and continues to laugh.

"What?" he asks.

I hold out my hand for him and he grabs ahold of it and pulls himself up. I look out to where the car crashed. He turns his head and surveys the damage.

"We fucked that all up to hell, didn't we?" he asks and I nod back.

We can already see the passing shadows of more and more monsters coming to inspect the damaged door.

"Well, they know we're here now, don't they?" I ask him.

He stares back at me and then spits on the ground. "Yep."

"Who's gonna tell Kel?" I ask.

He turns back to me, smiles and says, "It was your plan. I was just along for the ride."

"I knew you would say something stupid," I say back to him. We move around the front of the car and I have to practically stand on the hood of the car to open the door. Before we make it into the stairwell, we hear something hit the door. It sounds like a fist.

10.

"What the fuck did you two do?" asks Kel as she gets up from behind the desk.

Scott instantly flops down on the couch and begins to put his password into the screen from the night before. I look down at him and then join him on the couch. Scott turns to me and smiles.

"What do you mean?" I turn back to her and ask.

"What the fuck do you think I mean? I mean what the fuck did you two think you were doing?" she says making her way over towards us. She looks like a mother who just found her kids carving dirty words into their neighbor's car.

"We had a little run in," I say back. Scott snorts and then tries to stifle a laugh. Kel moves in front of the screen, turns around and turns off the game.

Scott and I both say, "Hey," and then realize that we shouldn't have said anything.

"Hey-fucking-nothing. I watched your little adventure in the garage on the vid-feed." She walks over and taps the screen and a still-frame of two headlights comes up on the television. Damn, she's good.

"Let me jog your memory," she says and then taps the screen twice and the headlights shoot forward and then swerve into the door. She taps the screen once more and the image of the Focus rammed into the steel roll down door is frozen on the screen. "You couldn't have just shot them?" she asks.

Scott looks over to me and then back up to her. "We freaked. Sorry."

"Yeah, no shit you freaked. You ran a car into one of the only things that is holding a city full of fucking monsters from getting into the building."

I hold my hand up to interrupt and she moves from staring daggers at Scott to staring huge swords at me.

"What, asshole?"

"If you saw everything go down, why didn't you help us and turn on the lights so we could see?" I ask.

She brings her arms up as if she's going to strangle me and then crosses them over her chest and says, "Because by the time I found the command for the lights, you two were already done alerting everything inside and outside the building that we're here."

"We panicked, Kel. Yeah, we messed up, okay? But the car works and the door is still holding, right?" says Scott. He's holding the controller to the Nintendo in his hands as if he can use it to advance the conversation forward.

"Yeah, well let's just fast forward to when you two assholes left the garage, shall we?" she says and then drags her index finger across the screen. I watch as muzzle flashes and violence erupt like live concert footage. I watch the two of us clamber over the hood and get through the door. She stops at a point that's just about five minutes past when we've left and points to the garage door.

"Here, look." She taps the screen again and the vid-feed keeps rolling. Through the slivers of what appears to be pure white rimming the door, we see shadows begin to multiply. Then the door begins to shake. At first it looks like someone outside threw something against the door.

It shakes violently once, then twice and then as more seconds and minutes go by, the door begins to look more and more like it's footage from an earthquake. The roll steel ripples like water from the continual abuse it's under.

"Now, look outside," she adds. Scott and I reluctantly get up from the couch and make our way towards the windows and look down.

Below us is an undulating sea of crooked monster bodies. All of them are trying their hand at slamming into the garage door. I look further up the avenues that surround the building and out towards Public Square. For whole city blocks, almost as far as the eye can see, there are bodies approaching. Like an army of hungry ants or a rotten tributary of filth, they filter down and through the streets towards the increasing noise of the already incredible amount of bodies outside of the building.

"It's not just on the door side either," she says and then spins the garage footage across the screen and taps out another command to bring up the building's exterior security cameras. Along the entire base of the building, the army of monsters is advancing and growing, with more and more of the new arrivals adding layers to the hordes.

"What are we supposed to do about that?" she asks.

Scott leans his head into the window, closes his eyes and whispers, "Shit."

I stand up straight and look out towards the horizon. The fires seem to have died down a bit. Maybe they are running out of fuel. Though that's impossible, there are still enough abandoned buildings and homes and new construction to fuel a thousand more fires. Maybe this is just the eye of the storm? I turn around and make my way towards my desk, sit down, pull my cigarettes out and light up.

"Did you find anything in here?" I ask her as I motion for the screens to come alive again. The security feeds are up and running and I tap them away and restore control of the television to a blank channel for Scott to use.

Kel shakes her head in frustration and then moves back towards the desk and says, "Yes."

She leans over my shoulder, careful not to touch me, but something in her body language tells me that she's come to terms with the fact that what I said before might be true. I'm hoping she found something on the servers that confirms my theory. She pulls up a blank white command prompt and taps out a couple of commands. She smells better and better the more I'm around her.

"Here, I found a couple of different things that might actually make me believe you were half-right," she says. Then she flicks her thumb and index finger open on the screen which magnifies the PDF file the commands brought up.

"What is it?" I ask her and she leans away from me.

"What, you can't read?" she replies.

"You already read it, so just tell me," I say back.

"Fine. It's a report that was still on a ghost server somewhere in your R and D department. It has some very nasty looking chemical formulas on it.

"This one here…" she says and then moves around to the other side so that she doesn't have to lean over me. "This one is actually a cache of emails that McMillan and your lawyer sent to each other about a 'Project Mobile' being scrubbed. They're pretty nondescript, but if you put what your little theory is all about into the mix, they make a little more sense."

"Like what?" I ask.

"Like the fact that, because you blew the doors off of Project Mobile at that press conference, they started working double-time on those formulas, which seem to be some new kind of biological weapon made from something called *Ophiocordyceps unilateralis*."

"English," I say back to her and she looks at me as if I've just tested her last nerve.

"From what I could find on your archives of the internet, it's some kind of parasitic fungus that's like 48 million years old that, to quote the article…" She pulls up a static page with an old highlighted article from some of my scientists. " '…evolved the ability to control the creatures they infect in the distant past, even before the rise of the Himalayas. The fungus grows inside the ants and releases chemicals that affect their behavior. Some ants leave the colony and wander off to find fresh leaves on their own, while others fall from their tree-top havens onto leaves nearer the ground. Scientists are not clear how the fungus controls the ants it infects, but know that the parasite releases alkaloid chemicals into the insect as it consumes it from the inside.' "

Scott stops inputting the password and looks over at us. "See? I told you, fucking zombies."

Kel and I look back at him and then to each other and back to the screen.

"That would explain the black goo stuff; it's fungal," I say bringing up the vid-feeds from outside and the garage again.

"Yeah, and it also explains why they attack; they're trying to spread the bacteria or fungus or whatever," she says while fumbling for her own pack of cigarettes.

She lights one up and then moves into the kitchen and grabs a cup of cold coffee.

"Question is," she says from the kitchen, "where the fuck are we going to go from here?"

* * *

We eat another meal of green beans, corn, rice and canned chicken. I don't eat as much as I did the night before, mostly because of what happened in the garage and partly because I had breakfast. Scott shoves mouthfuls of food into his face and goes back for seconds. I don't know why he cried today, or why he went on his berserker rampage, or how he can even eat after punching what used to be a man's head in, but I think that he's actually becoming someone I trust. Kel too.

I take the time after dinner to shower, shave and put on a fresh suit and brush my teeth. I look into the mirror after rinsing my mouth out and stare into my face. It's incredibly pale and my eyes are still fairly deeply set in my head. The bags under my eyes look more blue than purple and my bald head is starting to grow little 200-grit sandpaper-fine protrusions.

My hand trembles as I touch my cheeks and where some of the old acne scars are actually all healed up. Before I was frozen I didn't have the best skin, but it was actually getting better. I still had acne at thirty, but it was something that I was dealing with. Now I have a seamless and nearly smooth set of cheekbones. I haven't coughed in a while and though I really don't know if the treatment for the cancer worked or not, I don't feel like shit. Okay, I do, but it's a different kind of shit. There are no more little crow's feet at the corners of my eyes; there aren't any frown lines running down the sides of my mouth and if I haven't found the cure for cancer, then I think I found the fountain of youth.

After I come out of the bathroom Kel decides to take a shower and I show her where the towels and things are. I even show her where some of Janet's leftover hair and make up supplies are.

I walk over to the bar and pour a glass of Bushmill's and then flop down on the couch next to Scott. I watch as Simon Belmont moves in to slay Frankenstein's Monster and after the whiskey makes me feel brave I decide to ask Scott about Kel. "So, you and Kel—" I say before he gets out a no.

I look at him and then back to the screen. "No, what? No, you guys aren't together or no, I shouldn't ask?"

"Both," he says back without looking at me.

I start to apologize, "Okay, I was just—"

"Dude, I know what you were 'just' and the answer is no to both. Kel's not my type and I'm not hers. We went through basic together, she lost someone in the outbreak and so did I. leave it at that," he says.

"I wasn't asking because…" I begin to say but he pauses the game and turns towards me.

"Yeah, you were. I wasn't as high up as Kel, but I was spec ops, even if I was just a weekend warrior. I'm also a dude; I know what you're doing, the way you're looking at her now. Like now that you know she's an ace with a computer, she's not beneath you. I'm not retarded, man, I just don't talk much. Just drop it."

I turn back to the television to avoid looking at him. He turns back and un-pauses the game.

"So, what are we gonna do about that outside?" I ask trying to change the subject.

"No clue," he says as he shrugs his shoulders. "But if you don't stop talking, I'm going to punch you in the face. You did all right by me today in the garage, but I'm still not convinced you're not a monster."

I take a sip from my glass, stare into it and then get up and move towards my desk. I pull up the vid-feeds from outside, sit down in my chair fumble with my pack and pull out a cigarette. The sun has already gone down, fires on the horizon are back to being the only illumination outside the building besides starlight. The cameras have infrared and I can see the massive group of bodies ebbing and flowing around the building and, even at night, more and more are arriving. I stare into the screens and then up at Scott. The water in the bathroom stops and after a few minutes Kel comes out. I don't bother looking up when she comes around the corner from the doorway.

Scott gives a whistle and then says, "You clean up real good, Kel."

"Fuck you, asshole," she says back and then comes over to the desk and leans in to look at what's on the screen.

"You two really fucked shit up today, didn't you?" she asks me. I don't bother to answer the question.

I begin to say something, but when I look up she's staring at me, her eyes like shimmering cobalt, her wet hair smells like a mix of woman and my shampoo so I stop, close my mouth and turn back to the screens.

"That's a first," she says pulling her hair into a tight ponytail.

"Consider it the last. Anyway, what the fuck are we going to do about this?" I say and point to the screen. The ever-increasing numbers of bodies continue to collide into each other and bounce around the street like pinballs.

"I think you'll want to play the video from McMillan," she says and brings the screen with his paused faced on it to life.

Scott lets out a monumental "Yee-haw" as Simon Belmont finally destroys Frankenstein's monster. It begins to explode from the inside; swirls of yellow and orange explode from its body. Its legs drop off and explode, followed by its arms, and then finally its head explodes.

I take a deep breath and look into Robert McMillan's beady and evil eyes, and then tap the screen to continue playing the video. Robert McMillan sputters into life and begins.

"My fellow Americans, if you can hear me, or are seeing this message via global satellite, then I am Robert McMillan, the new President of the United States of America."

Whiskey and food begin to pile up in the back of my throat and I have to take another drink just to keep everything I ate from coming out.

"As you all know, many of the states and cities and communities that you are currently in have come under attack by what we believe to be a chemical and biological agent that is

causing those infected to quickly die and then come back to life with only one apparent goal: to spread the disease."

I want to stop the video, grab the screen and toss it out the fucking window. I want to find a way to time travel back to the day that he came to visit me and, even if he had an army of roided-out suited ape-men, shoot him in the face. I turn away and look back towards the lumbering and violent mass of bodies trying to get into the building.

"*But I have good news. After many months of planning and fighting, we've established several safe zones around the country.*"

I quickly turn back to the screen; Scott pauses his game to get up and walk over.

"*The following is a list of safe and secure locations that, if you are listening to or watching this, I pray you are able to make it to.*"

I watch as he signs off with a teary-eyed "*May God bless you, and may God bless the United States of America.*" The screen fades to black and scrolls the list of secure zones.

I pause the screen when I see the location that is closest to Cleveland: *Camp Perry: Port Clinton, Ohio.*

ERIC POLLARINE

PART THREE

1.

"So, we're going then?" asks Kel.

I can't say that I blame her for being skeptical.

"I'm going. You two can come along if you want," I say back to her as I start to pack a messenger bag full of underwear and toiletries. I figure it's roughly eighty miles or so to Port Clinton; I have it mapped out on a piece of copy paper. We've been having this conversation since Kel and I figured out that the messages weren't automatically sent. Someone must have seen us power up and log on to whatever was left of the satellite networks.

Scott is still trying to finish out the last level on *Castlevania*, but every once in a while he pauses the game and interjects. "Dude, you don't even know if that base is still operational," he says trying to get up the steps on the screen so he can finally face Dracula one-on-one.

"Look," I say, "we don't have enough food or water to last us a lifetime here." I put my toothbrush away in the bag and then decide against packing it up just yet. I can always grab it in the morning before I leave.

"Yeah, but we have enough for right now," Kel starts to say but I don't let her finish.

"We can't stay here. You guys can't stay here, and I can't stay here. We don't even know how much power—here—has left," I say. It's a blunt enough statement to make Scott get up and look at me like I just told him his dog, his mother and his fiancé just died.

"What the fuck do you mean? The other day you said—"

"The other day I said we have enough and the other day you were both holding guns to my head, so, you know, I may have lied."

I inspect a stick of unopened deodorant and then start to put it away in the bag when Scott rushes towards me. I look up to see a massive wall of anger coming straight at me and I barely have enough time to try and raise my arms and brace for the tackle. He slams into me and we hit the floor and both bounce. Pain shoots up and down my spine; he flies over me and rolls out a few inches away.

Kel starts yelling something, but before she can reach out to stop him, he grabs hold of my shirt collar and pulls me back down to the floor.

"What the fuck is wrong with you, man? Are you seriously the biggest asshole in the world?" he yells at my face. Little flecks of spit hit my mouth and I move to try and wipe them away. Skinny Scott pushes my hands down at my sides, but Kel grabs him before he can hit me.

"Scott, get off him," she tries to say, but he snaps at her.

"No, Kel, he needs to learn that he isn't the fucking world anymore," he says and shakes her off.

I watch as he pulls his fist back and my mind instantly jumps to the replay of him slamming his hand through the head of one of the monster men in the garage. This is going to suck, tremendously.

"He never was," she says as she slaps him across the head with her hand.

We both look up and say, "What?" then he pivots his waist around and looks at her like a confused child. Scott gets up and I shimmy out and pull myself up.

"Thanks, but what the fuck are you talking about?" I say back to Kel, but she just stares back at me for a while.

"You're welcome," she says finally, and then ads, "You might want to sit back down now."

I look around and then pull my chair from behind the desk and sit. After a few long seconds of staring, Scott moves his way back towards the couch. He sits back down, lights another cigarette and un-pauses the game.

"You're right: you're not a monster. You're a patsy," she says.

She looks at me as if she's about to tell me something massive. I hold up my hand, move to the bar and fix myself another four fingers of Bushmill's, then move back and sit down in the chair light a cigarette and say, "Proceed."

She frowns for a second and then says, "You're not a monster; you're just someone they could use. Jeff, you never even had cancer. McMillan was supplying you pills that kept giving you bronchial infections to make you think you were dying. He was just using you. He had you spotted and pinned ever since you started the company."

I feel my eyes bulging out of my head; I feel my blood pressure go up; I feel the rock glass slip through my hands, see it fall to the floor and then hear it break. My cigarette is hanging limp on my lips. I move to pull it away so I can ask for an explanation, but it pulls away a small piece of flesh and the raw spot burns for a second so I say nothing.

"Your whole company, all your money, your marriage…everything was a lie. Robert McMillan planned everything out, the funding for your app, your business decisions, your contracts. Your whole life, Jeff, was a complete lie. And when you started to get too big for your own good, do things that they couldn't control or predict, they wanted to get you out of the way, so they told you that you had cancer because they figured you would do something stupid."

I'm listening but I'm not. I hear what Kel has to say but I don't. I'm staring at her, watching her small lips move, her hair as it shakes slightly with her head. The hurt and pity in her eyes as they gleam out at me like emotional tractor beams, trying to reel me in and tell me she's sorry. But I don't actually listen, or hear, or see anything except my life flashing in front of my eyes.

Living and starving in my first apartment with Janet and talking to her father about the app, him introducing me to potential investors. The puppet companies for McMillan, the funds they miraculously raised for me to develop the app. I'm watching the shaking hands, the broad, knowing smiles pointed like knives at my face. I'm seeing the wedding reception; McMillan was there, too, literally. He showed up and put a check into the money well we had made shaped like a tablet computer. 20,000 dollars' worth of a gift, signed *For a better future*.

I see the company on the cover of *Wired*, *Time*, *Newsweek* and *Rolling Stone*. I see Phil coming to represent me; the carnivorous eyes of the dead on the screen to my left were nothing compared to Phil and Janet and McMillan. My doctor's initial tests and the diagnosis, the idea of cryogenics, the immortality they promised me. But it wasn't the immortality I wanted. I'm the man who ended the world. Now I am become Death, the destroyer of worlds, and McMillan gets to stand like the risen fucking Christ. I slump forward a little and bring the cigarette up to my mouth and stare at the glass on the floor, then over to the deodorant.

"Jeff, I'm so sorry," she starts to say but I hold up my hand and stop her. I think about what she said while I pick the deodorant up off the ground and then get up and start packing again.

"What are you doing?" she asks.

"I'm leaving," I say back, but my voice is hollow and far away.

"But what Scott said earlier is right; we don't know what the state of that base actually is. We just know that someone is there."

I stop packing and look up at her; the vacancy signs in my eyes make her take a step away from me, as if she's afraid.

"I'm going to leave, find McMillan, and then I'm going to kill him," I say.

Kel takes another step back. I know she thinks I've lost it, that I've snapped, but I haven't. In fact, I've never been more certain of anything in my life, ever.

"And what if he's not—what if he's already dead?" she asks.

"I'm pretty sure he's alive," I say and point at the screen that still has the Port Clinton location pulled up on it.

"You have no idea—"

"But we know someone is there, so they should know where he is and, like I said, I have no idea how long the power is gonna hold. Besides, look at it outside. You said it yourself: we fucked up."

We both look at the screen we dedicated to the cameras since Scott and I rammed my Focus into the main garage door. The massive tidal waves of bodies are still surrounding the building, smashing into the doors and windows with their hands. Every once in a while a large section of the group will turn their faces towards the sky or the cameras, and look right at us, though I don't think they're doing it on purpose. From what I can tell, they have no idea what's going on outside of the new instinct to spread whatever it is that they are supposed to spread.

"I know, but look at them," she says. "There's just too many of them for us to even attempt an escape."

I look at the screen again the deluge of bodies coming to the building has turned into a slow trickle, but they keep coming nonetheless. If I had to take a guess I would say there are already close to five thousand out there, maybe more.

"I know, but my Focus is—" I start, but this time Kel stops me.

"Your Focus is as close to a tank as we could possibly get, I know, but still—it's just a car. I've seen ten of those things overturn a car twice your Focus's size."

"Then we'll have to distract them, won't we?" I ask, and she gives me another look that says she thinks I've lost it. I'm starting to think she only has that look.

"And just how do you suggest we do that?" she asks.

So, up until now, I pretty much figured that I would just leave. As stupid as that sounds, it was my plan. I had actually forgotten that there was a mass of bodies waiting to tear us apart if we tried to leave. I stop packing more clothes into my second messenger bag and look up at her, and then over to Scott. He looks like he's calmed down a little or, at the very least, he's lost himself in the distraction of fighting Dracula.

"I don't know yet," I say back to her.

"So your plan was to just drive out there, where there are God knows how many of those things waiting, and what? Hope they didn't figure out how to tip the car over?" she asks.

"Pretty much," I say back as I finish packing the last of the two other suits that I want to take.

"I can't tell if you're the world's biggest asshole, or just the dumbest motherfucker I have ever met," she says smiling.

I stop packing, zip up the bag, look into her eyes and say, "Both."

2.

We're eating another meal of canned chicken, rice and mixed vegetables in silence. Kel keeps pushing the little white clumps of processed chicken around on her plate and making a dam that holds back her rice.

Scott eats like a ravenous animal and strips his plate clean twice. The guy's got an appetite no matter what; I almost envy him for his ability to compartmentalize what's going on. He's completely content with just playing games, drinking, smoking and eating. It's like the power isn't ever going to go out, it's like he's in shutdown from reality.

I look down at my own plate, already cleared but not enjoyed in the slightest and wonder if leaving is the right thing to do. We can't stay cooped up in here forever because, one, we have no idea as to how long the power is going to hold out, and two, as much as I want to deny it, I fucked us over by ramming the car into the garage door.

The horde of bodies hasn't grown since the last time I looked at the screen, but it hasn't thinned out any either. They slam their hands and fists into the building, the doors, the windows, anything in a pathetic attempt to try and figure out where the noise was coming from until all they have left are ragged stumps on the ends of their arms. If you are completely still and silent, you can hear their cries and moans coming from below; you can feel the small vibrations rattle up the insides of the building.

"I have to leave," I say to both of them but neither one acknowledges me right away.

Kel looks up from her half-finished construction site on the plate, sighs and then says my name in a way that reminds me of my mother. "Jeff, I know you're dealing with a lot right now," she starts to say but I stop the conversation dead in its tracks.

"No offense, Kel, but you have no idea what I'm dealing with."

I'm about to start tearing into her, but stop when I hear Scott.

"Let's fucking do it," he demands.

Kel and I turn and look at him; he's sitting back in his chair smiling and smoking a cigarette.

"What?" asks Kel. He leans in and takes a drink of water.

"It's just like *Castlevania*," he says, and then adds, "We're like Simon and McMillan's like Dracula. It's just something we have to do."

Kel shakes her head, then gets up from the table and takes our plates into the kitchen.

"I'm in," says Scott.

I don't know what to say, so I nod my head. Kel comes back over to the table and puts a beer in front of Scott and then opens a second one. I get up and get the bottle of Bushmill's.

"Okay," she says with a sigh, "How the fuck are we going to do this?"

* * *

We go back and forth for what feels like half the night. I look over towards the windows and the night sky is illuminated by the moon and stars. There isn't any light in the city except for the fires and my office, so the sky sparkles like a shattered jewelry store display case.

"Do we have any heavy ordinance left?" asks Scott.

"Nope," says Kel, "just a couple of clips for the pistols."

"What about you?" asks Scott and I pull away from space.

"The only thing I can think of is that they move in a crowd, so we could open the front doors to draw as many of them into the lobby as possible, then slam through the garage door and try to make it through the rest of them," I say.

"That might work," says Kel looking up from her beer. "How are we gonna open up the front door, though?"

"We could do it by remote from the Focus. It's networked to my office," I say back.

"Still gonna leave a fuck-load of 'em out there for us to try and get through, though," says Scott. We all nod our heads in agreement.

"You two don't have to come if you don't want to. We could secure the doors to the bottom floors and you could stay here if you wanted to."

Kel asks, "What are we gonna do when the power runs out? Or the food or—"

I shake my head to stop her from going on. "I was just saying it's not really your fight."

"It is now," says Scott, and I realize why he and Kel have made it this long.

"I think the door plan is as good as any," he says, then adds, "When are we doing this?"

"We should get as much food in as many bags as we possibly can into the car, get whatever else might be useful together and leave. So…one more day?" I say.

The gravity of the situation passes around the table as if it were a living cloud of doubt and acceptance. Each of us goes through the same set of faces and emotions as we think about the fact that tomorrow night will most likely be our last night on the face of the earth.

"One last thing," says Kel. I put my head down on the table. My hair has started to come back and it feels like a thousand separate pin pricks as I run my hand over my scalp.

"Yes?" I say from the tabletop.

"I'm sorry," she says. "Sorry for blaming you."

From the corner of my eye I see Scott nod his head in agreement. "Yeah, sorry, dude."

I pick my head up from the table and look at them to see if they're joking or not, but they both smile at me in the way that apologies demand awkward silences and I say, "Thank you," back to them in that weird way that acceptance brings relief.

We agree to go to bed and get as much rest as we can, try to sleep as long as we can, because we're leaving first thing in the morning exactly one day from now.

I lie in bed for another hour or so and stare out the windows. From the loft I can see the sky and the frozen light of the moon. I fall asleep to the slow and steady vibrations of the masses outside beating on the building and thinking that, whatever happens in the next two days, to those stars out there in the cold

THIS IS THE END

vacuum of space, none of this really matters because we're already dead.

3.

I wake up to the now familiar smell of coffee and cigarettes, biscuits and chicken. But as I come down the steps, the air in the office feels different. It feels as if someone opened a window, though I know that's totally impossible. Kel is cooking and Scott is staring out the window, the smog and clouds and grey have lifted from the surrounding area and the sky is a vast and clear expanse of cerulean. The sun beats down on him, and he casts a long shadow over the floor.

"Morning," he says as he hears me come down the metal stairs.

"Hey," I say back to him as I make a straight line for the kitchen. Kel is finishing up breakfast and I pour myself a nice huge cup of coffee.

"Hey," says Kel as I move to go back out towards my desk. I stop and look back and she smiles at me.

"Hey," I say back to her as well, and then she moves towards me.

"Jeff, I meant it last night when I said I was sorry. I just want you to know that."

"I know," I say and try to look at her through one half-opened, bloodshot eye.

"It's just that…" she starts and I take a long drink from my cup.

"I know, Kel, it's fine," I say back.

"Listen," she says and then pauses for a few seconds. "I modded your app right after it came out, and it really was a brilliant piece of code. It wasn't all McMillan and the rest; you built something one of a kind."

"Thanks," I say back to her and move to my desk, wave my hand in front of the screens and smile as they come to life.

I double tap the one that has the video from McMillan still paused and it minimizes down to the task bar. I scan the one that's monitoring the wall of bodies still trying to get at the insides of the building. The sunlight doesn't help the situation much; I can see their faces even more clearly than before.

Mouths hang slack and wide, blackened teeth and tongues loll about inside. Many of them raise their stumps up and continue to beat on the brick; ragged, rotten shreds of meat hang down and taper off in paper-thin shreds at the ends of their arms.

I don't want to admit it, but it's actually becoming easier to look at them, to scan the faces and empty eye sockets, the sickly sheen on their skin. It's all becoming more and more tolerable.

I open up the main controls for the building and then put it into hibernation. Other than getting food and supplies ready, we're pretty much done. Kel brings out three plates of food and we all sit down to eat. The meal tastes better than the others did, and I don't know if it's the sunlight or the finality of the plan to escape or what, but the morning seems to be nearly perfect.

I look around. Kel and Scott are laughing at something he's said; they're sitting close enough on the couch that, if you didn't know it was the end of the world, they would be two people who didn't know they loved each other.

I look over to window and the rays of light from the brilliant sun are defined by the clouds of cigarette smoke.

"Hey," I say and they both look up. "Does it feel...different to you?"

Scott shrugs his shoulders and fires back, "Calm before the storm—enjoy it."

Kel nods and then adds, "When it's the night before you drop into a hot zone, same thing happens. Tonight you'll have a ton of nerves if you don't just forget about it. Then tomorrow...well, it'll be pretty crazy."

I sit back in the chair and try to enjoy the rest of the morning.

* * *

Halfway through the afternoon we begin to get ready for tomorrow. Scott and I take a couple of pillowcases and several smaller suitcases that I found in my closet up in the loft and make our way down to the cafeteria. I had Kel cut power from the rest of the servers and non-essential systems and route it to the elevator.

After we make our way down to the cafeteria, we make sure to load up with everything from the pantry. The only things we leave are a couple of cans of franks and beans that said they went bad three years ago; if it had been just a year, we would have considered taking them.

Once we were done there we turned our attention to the beer cooler. After we were totally done we decided to take one trip to minimize the chance of making a ton of noise that would alert the mass outside.

The pillowcases are heavy and Scott has to take the majority of the load. As we walk back through the empty silence of the cafeteria, a shiver runs up my spine. When the world wasn't over—when it was just show up to work everyday and wait to find out what's playing on the television—this place was the hub of activity. A highly polished, multi-function workspace, now it's a tomb, a frozen memory of normalcy. Scott makes it to the elevator first and then realizes that I've stopped moving.

"Dude, what? Did you hear something?" he says putting down the two sacks full of canned food.

"No, no, I was just thinking about before," I say back.

"It's archeology," he says as he hits the down button and turns back around.

I pull the suitcase behind me and roll into the elevator. As the doors begin to close I nod my head. We're all archeology now.

* * *

The elevator opens directly across from the stairs so we'll have to be extra quiet when we exit. In the elevator Scott and I talk about video games and beers that we liked. He tells me about being from Akron and then moving down to Tennessee when he had initially signed up for the Army. He tells me about his time in Afghanistan and how, if you could get past the shelling, suicide bombers, snipers and the limbless women and children, it was actually a very scenic place. We swapped stories about quitting shitty jobs and first cars.

The elevator stopped and a big digital G popped on the screen above the door. I broke into the panel and cut the wires for the speaker so that the computer lady didn't blow our cover, but I knew somewhere there was a command being executed for the voice to say, "*Garage floor. Thank you.*"

The elevator doors slide open and instantly the smell makes us both gag. The garage door had become dangerously unstable and through the gap under the door we could see what looked like a dense forest of calves and feet in the midday sun. The noise from outside was enough to mask any small amount of noise that we could have made. After getting the hatchback open and shoving everything in, I get into the driver's seat and, careful not to actually start the car, turn on the systems. Scott stands outside in the parking garage and smokes a cigarette.

I make sure that we have a connection to my office servers and start tapping in commands to link the two. Kel pings in on the messaging system and does what she can on her end. In a matter of minutes we are up and running and ready to go; a little part of me really wants to leave now. The other part of me, the rational and sane part, wants to go upstairs, sit down and drink myself into a coma until the last sparks of power fizzle into nothingness. I push the pity into my guts and light up a cigarette. I message Kel that we're done and then turn the car off and get out.

"Jesus, man, listen to those fuckers out there," says Scott.

I stop and listen to the sounds of tiny thunderclaps rolling across the door and little bombs being dropped on the bricks outside. The longer I stare at the door, the more convinced I become that it's going to give way at any second. I close my eyes and breathe, the noise seems to intensify. I could stand here and be sucked into the off-timing and thrum. I can feel the small vibrations move through the concrete and travel up my legs, into my chest. Each beat says *Death, death, death.*

"Shit," says Scott and I open my eyes, shake my head.

"What?" I ask.

"I forgot a pillowcase by the elevator," he says and then moves back towards the nearly overflowing sack that's sitting outside the doors.

"Do you really think we need it?" I ask.

"Might as well. We don't know what else is out there or how long it's going to take," he says back.

I open the hatchback and try to make enough room. I pull out the road kit and open it up. There are a couple of flares, three collapsible reflective triangles, a set of cheap jumper cables and a poncho. I toss everything but the flares, which I shove into my back pocket.

We must have packed the case especially full because Scott has to drag it over to the back of the car. I grab one end and he moves around to the other and we lift in unison. We stop in unison when we hear the tear and watch in unison when the cans hit the concrete and cringe in unison as the noise of a sackful of cans makes its way above the din of banging. Both of us freeze in unison and watch a single, solitary can of green beans roll towards the gap in the garage door.

I hear my voice say, "Fuck," which, up until that point, was a near impossibility. Scott looks at me and I look at him and then we watch as the can of green beans clears the gap under the door.

"Totally," says Scott.

For a few seconds we don't know what to do, and then it hits us. The banging has stopped. The silence is nauseating and I feel a wave of bile and adrenaline flood up my body and into the back of my throat. The mass of feet and ankles and shins are still; the rolling waves of the metal door have stopped. The moaning and breathing have ceased and in the absence of the crowd, the vacuum of noise, there is only the sound of the can of green beans rolling back towards us underneath the door.

4.

The explosion of violence against the door rocks the two of us back on our heels. The door is shuddering in its track to the point that it nearly jumps off the frame.

"I think our plans just got bumped up a few hours," I say to Scott. He's already moving back towards the elevator doors.

"Yeah, I think you're right," he says while pushing the up button and pulling out his pistol.

I pull out my own gun from my waistband and then shake my head; it would be pointless to use them if the door bursts. We make it into the elevator and begin moving back up to my office. I click the intercom button and start to call for Kel.

"What the hell did you two do?" she asks from the other end. "They're going apeshit out there."

"Can of green beans fell out and rolled out the door, but now's not really the time, Kel. Get your shit; we've got to move," I say back.

There's a long silence on the other end, but I don't hear the click of the intercom. Scott looks at me and I shrug my shoulders. We hear movement on the other end of the speaker.

"You two are no longer allowed to do anything without me," she says back and then I hear the intercom shut off.

"I really hate green beans," says Scott.

"Me too," I say back as we make our way up to the office.

* * *

Kel is waiting in the lobby and the stench of rotting flesh is just as intolerable in here as it was in the garage. The bodies on the ground have begun to sink into themselves and already decay has started to work its way through the softer parts and bits of scarred flesh on their hands and faces.

"Here," she says while throwing Scott his backpack. It hits him in the chest and he lets out a gasp. After that she tosses in my two bags and she's already got hers on her back. I try to step out of the elevator and go back into the office when she grabs me by the back of my collar and pulls me back towards the elevator.

"What are you doing?" she asks.

"I have to—"

"I already packed up the smokes, coffee and two bottles of whiskey. What else do you need?"

I look back out towards the open doors and into my office. The stark white interior gleams in the late afternoon sun. Everything I have ever been, wanted to be and accomplished is staring back at me. Inanimate objects that were my friends and confidants, consoles and screens, oak flooring and unblinking glass eyelets look back at me coldly like a spurned lover. I open my mouth to protest, to say that I've forgotten something, but I haven't. This wasn't really me to begin with.

"Nothing," I say as I get back into the elevator and watch as the doors close. I stare at the spot on the door where my office doors would be as we move down towards the garage again.

"Hey," says Kel and then snaps her fingers in front of my face. I look over to here and then back to Scott, who's checking his ammo situation.

"What?" I say.

"I found this the other day," says Kel and then hands me my tablet.

My eyes go wide and I hold it like a newborn child. I thumb the power button and check the battery bar: fully charged. Good.

I tap the screen and it brings up a four-way display. One is the outside and I see the results of the can rolling under the door. Now that the things know something is in the building they have intensified their assault on the walls and doors. Another section is a display of the main unit upstairs, another is tied into the car and the last is everything that we received from Port Clinton and the documents about how everything happened.

"As you can see, I've patched everything into it. All we have to do is go," she says.

"Yeah, I see. Where did you find this?" I ask.

"Right after Scott and I got trapped in your office, we looked through everything. I found that in a coat of yours. Looks like they didn't think that you would ever come back from the dead," she says.

I smile and look down at the screen and thumb through everything again. The elevator comes to a stop and I look out as the doors are opening up. The doors are near the breaking point. Each blow to the roll steel pushes it into and out of its frame, putting us closer and closer to the ravenous mob outside. I hand the tablet back over to Kel as we move towards the car.

"Here," I say and then add, "My car—I'm driving. When we get in, open the doors to the building and get down in the seat."

She nods as we throw our gear into the backseat. Kel hands Scott her pistol and they exchange glances that say *I love you*.

When we're finally all in I start the car and say, "Okay, everyone ready?"

"Let's do it," says Scott and Kel smiles while crouching down into the floor well of the passenger seat.

"All right, open the doors."

Kel motions with her finger over the display and brings up the main control screen. She hesitates, takes a deep breath and then taps the button for the magnetic locks on the doors. I grip the steering wheel tightly and hold my breath.

"I hope this works," she says from the floor, "because if not, it's gonna be a real short drive."

5.

For the first few minutes after Kel tapped the screen, nothing happens. The doors all look the same. The waves of pounding fists on the outside of the garage doors continue. She brings up the external security camera feeds and watches as the things outside keep on as if nothing had happened. She pulls herself back up into the passenger seat and Skinny Scott sits upright in the back. We stare at the screen for a long while. The mood in the car rapidly goes from complete anxiety to utter despair. I sit back in my seat and look at the gap under the door. The thick mass of legs and ankles haven't moved.

"Shit," I hear Scott say from the back as he tries to slouch backwards into the rear seat.

Kel has brought the main controls back around with the flick of her fingers and started to double-check the command sequences for the doors.

"I triple-checked them," I say to her, but she doesn't register that I've said anything.

I roll my head back to look out at the door and fumble around in my suit jacket to find my cigarettes, but as I look down towards my pockets, I glance out the door and then stop.

"Hey, look." I point towards the gap and Scott leans forward and squints.

"There are less of them," I say and I can see Scott nod in agreement. Kel is still thumbing through commands, but pauses and looks up, then stops.

From underneath the door I start to see more concrete and more daylight, and then as we are watching, we see the first set of legs move towards the right hand side of the door.

"Hey, listen," says Scott.

Kel stops moving her hands and then pushes the down button for the window, only allowing a fraction of a gap between the window and frame, but it's enough to tell us that the pounding has subsided. It's still there, but it's subdued.

"Do you have the interior cameras tied into the feeds?" I ask Kel.

She flickers her fingers across the air in front of the tablet and pulls up the outside feeds.

"Holy shit," she says. "It's working."

She stretches the front camera feed to fullscreen and we see the deluge of bodies trying to cram themselves into the front doors of the building. She rewinds it back a few frames and we watch as one of the crooked men pulls at the door and in the next frame it looks like twenty more rip the door off its frame. After that it's like a meat grinder as the bodies try and move in unison towards the opening.

She brings up the feeds from inside the building and we watch the bodies move like a wave of destruction throughout the lobby and up the doors and through the hallways of the building's first floor.

"Um, I think we should go," says Scott from the backseat.

I look back at him, but only see the back of his head and the main door from the stairwell behind us bounce.

Once and I look back towards the garage door.

Twice and Kel looks back.

Three times and then door blasts open; the monsters smash out of the doorway like a wave of vomit.

"GO!" yells Kel.

I grab the steering wheel and floor the pedal. Kel and Scott slam back into their seats as we race towards the crooked door.

"SEAT BELTS, NOW," I yell back but it's too late; we're already at the point of impact.

For exactly five seconds it feels as if everything in the world is slow motion movie-still. I know it was exactly five seconds because before we hit the door I looked at the huge clock on my dashboard and it reads out hours, minutes and seconds.

The glass spiderwebs a little. The metal from the hood meets the metal of the garage door and makes the worst nail-on-chalkboard times a million sound. The door crumples up and out towards the remnants of the crowd just outside. Smaller, saucer plate-sized pieces of metal dislodge themselves from the side wall and become death Frisbees; some even find homes inside of the unsuspecting bodies outside.

Kel and Scott fly up and out of their seats along with some of our canned food, which for those few seconds look weightless, hovering in the air. Scott has the benefit of being in the back seat and slams his face into the back of Kel's seat. Kel is less fortunate and faceplants on the windshield; as she falls back towards her seat she leaves a small tracer line of spittle and blood from her lips.

The weight of the car against broken bodies outside is stomach-turning. After the fifth second passes the world seems to catch back up to us and everything jerks back into normal time. The sunlight outside blinds me for a few more seconds; I swerve into more bodies and then we're out. Kel slips down into her seat as if she's melting and Scott grabs her and pulls her back up.

I look over and start to ask, "Holy shit. Is she—" but Scott cuts me off with, "Just drive."

I haven't brought my foot up from off of the gas and we are rocketing forward towards the side of another converted warehouse building. We jump the sidewalk but I manage to crank the wheel all the way left and move us back out onto the actual street.

We smash into something with substance that crunches back. I look in the mirror and see we've just taken out a trash can. I watch it bounce back towards my building, but then the mass of bodies pouring out from all the openings of my building catches my eye. Some of them move faster, some of them move very slowly, others have a normal, almost living gate, but they are all after us.

I look forward and see a series of chained-together metal riot pens in front of us. I gun the car's gas pedal again and break through the shoddy line. The barricades upend and disconnect, leaving them to look like the leftover ribcages of some forgotten metal beast.

Kel is still slouched unconscious in the passenger seat, still holding onto the tablet. Scott is trying to bring her back around and getting odd bursts of consciousness from her.

I drive around Public Square, making sharp turns around the Soldiers' and Sailors' Monument, past the broken and torched front of the Terminal Tower, the entrance to Tower City Shopping Center, moving towards Ninth Avenue. More riot cages and barricades crumble as we blast through them. I have to jerk the Focus around from left to right to avoid hitting the scattered, abandoned cars. I try to shut out the sound of thuds and crunches as we roll over body bags that are stacked two and three high.

The screen on the tablet is cracked, but the display is still feeding us info on what is happening around the building, the security protocols are off the chart for breaches, but the servers back inside my office are still online.

Kel snaps back into coherence and bolts upright, throwing Scott backwards towards his seat.

"What happened—did we make it?" she asks.

"Yeah, but you smashed your face. We're out; where are the directions?" I ask while trying to avoid a stray, moving monster. I watch it turn around clumsily and reach out for us as we pass it in the rearview.

Scott lurches forward with a bottle of water and hands it to Kel. She takes a sip and then winces as the bottle comes back from her lip which is currently split into several parts and bleeding profusely.

"I uploaded them here," she says and taps the screen and the directions I wrote down appear on the screen. She hands me the tablet and I dock it on the dashboard.

"You okay?" she asks back to Scott.

He nods and says, "Yeah."

I stop the car when we get to the on-ramp for I-90 West.

"What are you doing?" asks Kel.

I point up towards the ramp. The freeway, the on-ramp, the section of the main road that leads up to the on-ramp, and the better part of "as far as the eye can see" are full of abandoned, broken, twisted cars stopped in both directions. I look into the rearview and make sure there's nothing immediately behind us and then get out of the Focus.

* * *

"What are we gonna do?" asks Scott. He's facing down Ninth Avenue with both guns drawn, scanning from left to right. Kel is trying to clip her bottom lip back together with a first aid kit she had in her bag. I'm standing on top of the Focus staring at the neverending line of cars in all directions.

"I don't know," I say honestly and look back towards him. "I didn't know it was like this," I add as I jump down from the hood.

"It's like this everywhere," says Kel.

"Well, we can't just stay here; they're going to spread back out into the city after us," says Scott.

"Well, it's not like we can go back, can we?" I ask him but he doesn't answer. I see his body tighten up.

"What is it?" asks Kel, but he turns back to us and shushes us.

We hear it before we see it, the sound of moans and wails and screams and feet—lots and lots of feet—as they echo around the empty buildings and alleys of the city. Then a wave of broken bodies begins cresting the small hill below us.

"I think we should get going," I say but Kel and Scott are already in the car waiting.

I start the car and move it into reverse, turn us around and head straight for the wave.

"What the hell are you doing?" asks Kel, but I concentrate on aiming the Focus straight ahead.

"Thinning out the heard," says Scott from the back while he scrambles to find his seatbelt. Kel clips in seconds before I smash headlong into the forefront of the surge.

Running over people, whether they are the walking dead, monster men, crooked creatures, the poor infected or whatever else you want to call them is just as gruesome, but not as easy, as you would think. We smack into the unfortunate thing that's just out in front of the rest of the mob and send it down and under the undercarriage of the Focus. The car shakes and my stomach turns with the dull thud and pop that must have been its head.

THIS IS THE END

The rest of the wave pools around us in a whirlpool of torsos, arms and faces. I had gunned the engine enough before we made contact that the Focus keeps moving, but I can feel the transmission lurching under the stress of giving it all it's got. The original specs on the car, if it were factory, would never have allowed it to get this far.

Faces slam into the windows with open mouths, rotten teeth and tongues, bloody, shredded palms and fists slap and beat at any part of the car they can get to. More bodies fall under the wheels; more strain is put on the driveshaft and bearings. The tires get caught on a body that's especially big and grind into it as if we were stuck in deep snow. They spin and shower blood and black goop onto the crowd behind us. I wrench the steering wheel left and right in an attempt to get more traction and finally jump the body. I try to spray wiper fluid over the windshield but one of the monsters gets hold of the right wiper blade and tears it off.

We smash through the back end of the crowd and move back into the city center.

6.

The Focus pushes forward steadily, but I can feel it starting to limp a little. If we get into another jam like that again, we'll be completely fucked. At this point I'm not even sure it's going to make it out of the city. Kel and Scott are on lookout, scanning every inch of open space for an exit.

"They bottlenecked all of them into the city center," says Kel. "They tried to move all the infected into the city center; they were going to wipe it off the face of the earth."

"Why didn't you tell us this theory when we were trying to figure everything out before?" I ask her while trying to avoid smashing into anything else in the road.

We've gone around the outskirts of the city several times and haven't run back into any more of them yet. But at this point it's just a matter of time before we circle back into the mass. I light up a cigarette and crack the window.

"I didn't know how bad it was. When we were flown in here to get you, the suburbs weren't as bad as the city center and even that wasn't as bad as this," she says.

I stare at the tablet's cracked screen; it's still running on satellite with the servers from my office, though even that is beginning to get spotty as we continue to move around. The satellites probably haven't been triangulated in almost a year and I'm surprised that they are still running as smoothly as they are.

"Try raising Port Clinton," I say to Kel.

She doesn't register for few seconds. "We don't even know that the messages were—"

"Just try," I add. She picks up the tablet from the dock and starts thumbing through the command prompts from the servers back in the office. After several attempts at logging into the network she gets through and taps out a couple of commands and messages. We continue to drive. She plugs the tablet back into the dock and looks out the window.

"Anything?" I ask and she shakes her head no. She moves her hand to her face and wipes at her cheeks. Scott puts his hand on her shoulder and she lays her hand on his.

"I put it on a loop; it'll generate a message every fifteen seconds."

We pass by a couple of armored troop carriers and Scott sits upright in the back.

"We should see if there's anything out there we can use." "Do you want to stop?" I ask and look back at him.

He surveys the ground and the carriers, then looks at me and says, "No."

I look back at him and then back towards the road one more time before everything goes white.

* * *

First it's white, then it's yellow, then red, then purple, then after a while there are slivers of sky and starlights in the daytime. At first it's nothing, then it's hot, very hot, then it's burning and you can't breathe and then it's rushing wind and your body is trying to suck oxygen into it at any opening. Then it's cold and black and that lasts for what seems to be an eternity. Then, if you're lucky, I assume you don't wake up. If you're as unlucky as I am, then you do.

* * *

The world is an acid trip. I have no hearing. I can't move my mouth except in an attempt to flood my scorched lungs with air. The buildings and concrete ripple with waves, whether real from the heat or imagined from the part of my brain that can still produce images is up for debate. Pain shudders through my body in long, tingly, serpentine spasms. I smell what I believe is burning flesh or hair or cotton. It could be all three; I can't really differentiate the odors from one another. This is the third time I have felt like this in my life. I need to figure out how to stop it from happening.

One way, says my brain: *don't drink whiskey laced with sedatives.*

Another way, my brain says: *don't freeze yourself if you think you have cancer.*

And the last way, my brain says is: *don't roll over landmines.*

I answer my brain back with, *Was the last one what that was?*

I try to pick myself up off the ground and manage to get on my feet before tumbling back down towards the ground. At least I put my arms out in front of me this time. At least this time it feels like I only shattered my left wrist as opposed to my entire frame.

I'm lying on my face, surrounded by open cans of creamed corn. There are cooked mixed vegetables falling from the sky and landing all around me. Some boiled potatoes to my right look like they have been flash-fried. The ringing comes back, like I've been to a concert and stood with both of my ears a few millimeters away from a speaker cabinet all night, a solitary sine wave tone in 360 degrees.

I'm smoking. Not cigarettes. I don't even know where those are right now. But me, my actual body, my suit, my shirt and hands are smoking. Like steam from a bath or fog in a swamp, I watch ghostly waves of white trail off of my fingers and arms. I look around and see the Focus. But that's not right. The wheels don't go up, the top doesn't go down, there should be doors and, at this point, though I could be wrong, the front shouldn't look like a flower that's just bloomed. I look around with my eyes because moving my head feels like I'm shaking a bowl of pudding.

Where's Scott and Kel? asks the small amount of me that's left. I see arms and hands, a pistol that looks melted to the ground.

I see our bags—well, the contents of our bags—splashed about in small piles of undergarments and disintegrated cigarette packs. Loose tobacco is everywhere.

I try and turn myself over and get onto my back. I manage to flop enough that I roll and stare up again into the fading light of the sky. I see a black cloud caterpillar rising into the sky from the tires on the Focus. There's blood in my mouth so I try and lick around the inside and find that there are two teeth nestled inside of my cheek. I bring my right arm up to my face and pull the teeth out.

The lonely wail in my eardrums is beginning to subside and for a split second, I could swear I hear someone that sounds like Kel crying.

I close my eyes for what feels like a few seconds, but could be hours, and when I try to open them again, I'm being dragged. The face melts from Kel to Scott to Janet to Phil to McMillan to Kel to Janet to Scott, to my father, to me, to Scott to…I close my eyes again. It's better this way.

7.

The air is cold and I'm shivering. I feel like I'm wet and something heavy hits my left eye as I try and open it. I don't know what's wrong with the right one, but it's not pulling its weight. It's raining. There are storm clouds in the sky, lightning flashes every second or so. Fucking Cleveland weather. There are little pellets of gravel underneath me; I try to move and my body tells me to just stay where I am. Don't be a hero. I'm captive to its whims.

I try to call out for Scott first, then for Kel, but there's no answer. It feels like the whole world is swaying and the wind is ripping at my clothes. I move my right arm as my left is useless, and fumble around inside my suit pocket for my cigarettes.

I pull out the pack and then look for a lighter but can't find one anywhere on my person. I pull open the pack and put one in my mouth anyway and suck back on it. Maybe it'll melt in my mouth.

I move my arm over to my other pocket where I felt the bulge and pull out what was in it. It's the tablet. The electromagnetic touchscreen is completely shattered. I balance it on my chest without putting too much pressure on my ribcage and try my thumb on the screen—motherfucking thing still works. It's still pinging messages to Port Clinton. That would've made a great pitch: "Will take a direct blast from a landmine." I smile and let it flop on my chest.

I move my head up enough that I can look around and notice that I am in the sky. Not literally, not floating, but I'm up high, high enough that I can make the tops of other buildings that are on the same level as I am. I look around and see a figure slumped over on the gravel. I'm pretty sure it's Kel; she looks bad. Her hair is singed and her face is scarred and bloody. Her left cheek is melted and drooping. There appear to be large protrusions coming out of her side; they look like the police riot cages but are grey and white and bloody instead of rusted and metal and silver. I try to say something to her, but I don't know what I could say. She's staring back at me and if it wasn't for the fact that she's blinking every once in a while, I would have thought she was dead.

She has a gun in one hand. The other is twisted in a way that could never be fixed. How the hell did she get me up here? Where are we? The thunder rolls above our heads; it sounds as if God and all the other angels in heaven are beating a garage door, like God and all the other angels in heaven are monsters.

Every time the lightning flashes she blinks, but she never stops staring, never moves her eyes.

I look at the gun and it's smoking. I wait for the next flash of lightning and see that there is blood and little bits of brain splattered against the brick behind her.

I was wrong; Kel is dead. The rain is pouring down on me.

* * *

I assume it's morning when I open my eyes again. I have no clue as to when I closed them, though, to be honest, I have no idea as to how long I've been up here, nor do I even know where up here is. I try to move my head and it hurts slightly less than I thought it would, so I try and move the rest of my body and it hurts just as bad, but this time I push through the pain and sit up.

I instantly want to puke but there's nothing inside me to puke, so I hold tight. I look out towards the other building tops but can't get my bearings so I crawl to the side of the roof and look over. I look down and see the husk of the Focus still smoldering. But then the sight of hundreds of broken monster bodies and faces staring up at me, waving their hands and arms up at me, grasping for me, makes me reel backwards and lay back down on the roof.

I look over to Kel's body and decide to crawl to her. When I get there I see that there is a large bite mark on her arm, and then another one on her broken shoulder. I try to raise my arm up and close her eyes, but that only works in the movies, so I tip her over and she thuds to the rooftop. I look around and then check her pockets and find a lighter. I pull out a cigarette from my pack and light up. It feels terrible and wonderful at the same time. I cough up a little blood but as the nicotine rushes my brain, I start to put the events back together. I don't bother looking back over the edge of the building because I know that if Scott would have survived, then he would be here, too.

I crawl back to where the tablet is lying face down on the gravel and pick it up.

Without the glass it's hard to read what the screen says. My right eye is still not working right either, so I close it and try to focus on the screen.

I drop the tablet when I finally make out the screen: *Centcom.sysadmin.virginia. Sending helicopter to last known GPS relay. Scheduled ETA: unknown. Make sign.*

I sit back down and look out towards the horizon, towards the jagged architecture of the building tops and see the smoke from the fires in the distance. I try to crane my neck around and look behind me. There's nothing but more of the same. My body tells me to stop turning around in circles by shooting pain up and down my torso.

I pick the tablet back up and try to focus on the screen again. Maybe I've lost it; maybe the explosion knocked something loose inside my brain and I'm putting words on the screen that shouldn't be there.

Centcom.sysadmin.virginia. Sending helicopter to last known GPS relay. Scheduled ETA: unknown. Make sign.

I look around the rooftop again: nothing. I put the tablet into my jacket pocket and then push myself up off the ground and walk towards Kel's body.

She's still staring up at me, her eyes locked in an expression of fear and pain. I look at the side of her head and the crater from where the bullet exited. The emptiness of her skull, the bite marks and the gun are all too much. I feel my throat start to close and my eyes well up with tears. I try to fight them back. I try to push everything down, deep inside, but can't.

The wind shifts gently and I fall back down to the rooftop. I'm crying and I can't stop. I'm screaming and I can't stop.

This is all my fault. I grab at her shirt, take in handfuls of the material and wrench it around into my fists. The monsters below are wailing with me, a choir of longing, a choir of death. I match their intensity with tears and curses. I curse everything. I curse the sky and God and the monsters, Robert McMillan and, most of all, I curse myself. I let go of her shirt and grab the gun. I move towards the edge of the roof and peer over again.

I fire a round into the crowd and hit one of the monsters in the shoulder and it goes down, only to come back up a few minutes later, completely unaware that it doesn't have a shoulder anymore. Bone and rotten flesh, black goop and blood pour out of the wound. I fire again and again and again into the crowd.

I manage to take two of them out with lucky headshots. I'm not aiming, I'm reacting, and I'm wasting bullets. I stop and look up towards the sky. The sun is so bright; it beats me with its intensity. It bores a hole in me with its light. I stare into it through tears and I raise the gun up and fire. I want this to end. I want the sun to die and the earth to grow cold and the buildings to come crashing down onto the street.

The monsters beat at the sides of the building and windows and doors. I stand back up and limp around to the other side of the rooftop. There's a small lid that looks like it's a box top. I try to pry it up, but it doesn't move—must be locked from the inside.

"How the hell did we get up here?" I ask the air, looking back to Kel's body. But there's no reply.

I scan the edges of the roof again and then see the metal ladder of the fire escape.

"Why did you save me?" I ask back to Kel's body. There's still no reply.

I limp over to the front of the building again and look back down. The sea of bodies undulates and ripples like a tsunami. Bodies swirl around the perimeter like a vortex. Their venomous eyes stalk me; their hungry rotten mouths click-clack open and shut at me. The moaning makes me want to rip my ears off. I press my hands and the gun up to my ears to try and drown out the sound; I get the sound of the moans and something that sounds like the ocean. But there's something else. In the distance, underneath the sound of the monsters and the stillness of the city and ocean, it's rising rapidly. The distinctive *thump thump thump*, the staccato beating of rotors.

In the distance I see the pregnant belly of a black helicopter.

8.

I make my way over to edge of the building and try to wave my arms as I watch the helicopter make its initial pass through the city. Every time I move my shoulders it feels like they pop in and out of their sockets. I look around at the sea of pea pebbles and gravel on the roof, but there isn't anything up here that would burn, except for Kel's body.

I shake the thought from the inside of my head slowly and look down. The monsters staring up at me have moved on to trying to find the sound of the helicopter. The motors and blades slice through the silence of the dead city like a song that's skipping. I look down at the pistol in my hand and then pull the clip out. Just three shots left. I can't waste any more of the bullets.

I pull out my cigarettes and the lighter I got from off of Kel and light up; it's the only thing I can do as I watch the helicopter make another pass around the roof of a building two blocks over. I stand up on the small concrete lip of the building. The monsters come back from looking around to looking up at me. The moaning and wailing intensifies with their collected frustrations at not being able to get to me, and then changes; they're trying to find out where the noise of the chopper is coming from.

I look down into the sea of faces and wrecked limbs and, for the first time since I woke up, the first time since I encountered them, I realize that they have it better off. Isn't that always the plot in these things, these kinds of stories, the predictable monster movies like the one that I watched the other night starring some acne-scarred, rat-headed kid? The one I'm living.

I envy their inability to know, I envy their fortune and, most of all, I envy the fact that they have one collective drive. I slip back off the ledge and shove the gun into the gap between the small of my back and my pants; the barrel hits something in my back pocket.

I reach around into my back pocket and then pull out a single flare.

I went through a very long phase where I didn't believe in God, and then I went through a phase where I did and thought He had the worst sense of humor ever. Right now, I believe in God, and He's a vengeful, spiteful God.

I pull the plastic off the top, flip it around and watch as the helicopter makes another pass around where my building is. I look at both of my hands; they're shaking so much I don't even have to strike the top of the flare. The two ends make contact and the tiny sparks ignite and tear through oxygen, bringing a red blade of fire and smoke into life. The smell of sulfur pushes its way up to my face. I move back to the ledge and back into position at the lip of the edge. I wave it a few times in the air but my shoulders are still protesting any movement above my chest. The helicopter sweeps out wide and then back towards the lake as it sets its sights on the flare. I hold it high in the air despite the pain and signal it again. It dips its rotors once and makes one more pass around my building and then heads towards me.

The monsters below are furious; the wailing escalates to epic proportions. I can barely hear the crackling of the flare; I can barely hear my own breathing. The helicopter makes its way and then does a wide turn around to gain altitude. It's one of the big black Seahawk-model choppers, ugly and utilitarian. I look out towards where my building is, then down at the riot below as I'm stepping back from the ledge. The monsters are tearing each other apart trying to figure out a way to get to me.

The helicopter starts dropping altitude and I can feel the downdraft push on the top of my head. I instinctively crouch down. My back and knees begin to protest. My thighs and groin are nearly as bad, but I move out of the way and try not to put my hands on top of my head to hold down my non-existent hair. The flare is growing hotter in my hands as I watch the side door of the helicopter open. I half-expect to see more monsters, but the silhouette of a soldier pops out from the opening and he waves me to move off to the side.

He drops down the cable and it hits the rooftop with tremendous force. The massive noise of the helicopter's blades isn't enough to drown out the monsters as they try to crawl their way up the side of the building. Every time one gets to another's shoulder height, one of the others in the crowd rips it back down into the massive pile. I smile at the irony and move towards the cable. The same soldier's silhouette makes a motion for me to move back out of the way and then he swings out over the side and begins repelling down the cable.

He touches down on the pebbles of the roof as silent and careful as a cat, and then he moves towards me. I back off a bit, but he holds his hands open and pulls off his helmet.

"Sir, my name is Lieutenant Thomas Cooper, United States Army. I'm here to rescue you. Are you injured?"

I look at the dark-haired man and I want to call him Scott. He's about the same height and has similar features. My mind starts to index Scott's face over top of this soldier. I blink a few times to push Scott's memory back down and then I move towards him so I don't have to yell as loud.

"My name's Jeff. And probably," I say.

"Yes, sir, I know who you are. 'And probably' what?"

The Lieutenant's statement surprises me, so I ask him, "How do you know me?"

He looks at me for a few seconds and then surveys the horizon before turning his eyes back on me to answer.

"You were *Time* magazine's Man of the Year, sir. Are you injured?"

"Oh, yeah...that. And, yes, I think I drove over a landmine," I say back.

He takes the time to look around one more time and then spots Kel's body lying on the rooftop.

"Is there anyone else, sir?"

I shake my head and say, "No."

He nods and then begins hooking himself up to the cable again, but this time it's with clips and D-rings the size of saucers. The helicopter wobbles in the air above us. The wind and downdraft are nearly unbearable and my legs feel like they are going to give out on me at any moment.

"Are you able to hold on to me, sir?" he asks, motioning me to come towards him. I limp up next to him and he puts his helmet back on.

"I think so," I say back and he moves to grab my arms, but stops.

"What is it?" I ask him and he points at my hand.

"The flare, sir. You'll need to drop it."

"Oh, sure," I say.

I hadn't even noticed that the flare was still in my hand. It was getting hotter and hotter as the paper and sawdust and nitrate moved closer and closer to my fingers. Maybe I can't feel pain anymore, either. I look to the edge of the roof and then toss the flare over the side. The monsters roar over the helicopter's motors. He moves in, grabs me and then places my hands around him in a bear hug.

"Okay, hold on tight," he says, then he tugs the line and the cable moves from slack to tight in seconds.

I grip him in the embrace as our feet come off the rooftop and we move towards the opening in the side of the helicopter. After a few seconds I can feel my grip start to loosen; my arms are burning with pins and needles and great shooting knives of pain at the strain of holding on to the Lieutenant. The helicopter wobbles again and we start to spin as we ascend into the sky. As we turn I see Kel's body and I start to hug the soldier tighter. As we move closer to the opening I can see her body fading away. I hold the soldier tighter and tighter—forgetting all about the pain in my arms as they protest—bury my head into his shoulders and I start to cry.

We spin a few more times until the lip of the helicopter becomes my new horizon. I feel the arms of another soldier tear me away from the Lieutenant, but I don't want to let go; I don't want them to see me this way. I hear the soldier that's trying to pull me into the opening yell something but all I want to do is hug the Lieutenant and cry. I try to reach out to him but my muscles are shot. I can barely hold my arms up, let alone reach out forward to the Lieutenant. I'm finally ripped away by the other soldier and dragged up and onto the floor of the chopper. I watch as the other soldier moves on to helping the Lieutenant into the opening. Once we're both in, the Lieutenant unhooks from the cable and drags me back away from the opening.

I don't fight them when they pull me up and prop me into one of the seats; I don't resist when they pull the seat belts and harnesses around me. I can't...I can't stop crying. I can't stop looking out and down towards where Kel's body is. The Lieutenant tells the other soldier to strap in and then sits down next to me and double-checks my harnesses. I don't register that he's saying anything to me until we're already circling back around the top of the building.

"You're exceptionally lucky, sir. We gave up on finding survivors in Cleveland months ago," says Lieutenant Cooper.

I try to answer but can't; my Adam's apple is a rock in my throat and prevents me from speaking. The tears flow down my cheek and I start to feel faint. I watch as we gain altitude and Kel's body fades into the pointillism of the rooftop. She's beginning to disappear into the background colors of the pebbles: fleshtone, grey, purple, brown, bone and blood. Lieutenant Cooper moves towards the door and slides it closed. I look over at him as he sits down next to me again. I pull my arm up, wipe my snot onto the sleeve and try to clear my throat.

"I'm not lucky, Lieutenant. If I were, I'd be down there," I say and point towards where the rooftop should be.

He looks over to the door and then stares at the floorboards of the helicopter.

* * *

I stare at the door of the helicopter and imagine the monsters and destruction of first the city and then the suburbs. I look up into the helicopter's cockpit to try and see if I was right, and I can see the fires on the horizon, all this time, were homes in the first tier ring of suburbs. The second rings and tiers didn't fare any better. When we start to pass outside of the southeastern suburbs, I take notice of less immediately familiar landscapes. Lieutenant Cooper has been staring at the floorboards the entire time. The other soldier that pulled us into the helicopter is asleep. I move to look at Lieutenant Cooper.

"We're heading south?" I ask.

He snaps back nervously from his half-sleep and looks around the cabin of the helicopter, then to me and smiles. "Sir…yes. We're headed south."

"I thought you guys were out of Port Clinton," I say, then start to add, "The messages said that—"

"Port Clinton fell. We're from Virginia, sir," Lieutenant Cooper says over me.

"Is that where we're headed?" I ask him and he nods back.

"Yes, sir. We have orders to return," he says.

"Isn't that a little far for a helicopter?" I ask.

He nods his head. "We modified the chopper with an extra fuel tank." He then adds, "We have enough fuel to make a roundtrip flight."

"Who gave the order to come get us—me, then?"

He looks back out towards the sleeping soldier as if he wants the man to wake up so we can change the subject. He looks back to me after a few more minutes of beaming death rays at his partner. "The President, Sir," he answers.

"McMillan?" I ask.

"Yes, sir. The President," he says, nodding his head in agreement.

I bring my hand up to my face and wipe away the salt and dirt from my face. "Do you have any water onboard? I'm thirsty."

"No, sir. Supplies are very low," he says back to me.

"You smoke?" I ask him.

"No, sir—not anymore. There's no more cigarettes to smoke," he says.

I pull out my pack and flip the top up. I have three-fourths of a crumpled pack, so I pull out two and hand him one that doesn't look too badly damaged.

He smiles and says, "Thank you," as if the cigarette was encased in gold. He waits for me to finish lighting up to grab at the lighter. After the first couple of drags he looks like he's going to puke.

"You gonna be all right?" I ask him and he smiles as he exhales.

"It's been a while, sir," he says

"I bet," I say.

We finish the cigarettes in the relative silence of the cabin. After I stub out the butt on the floor, I let the ambient noise of the rotors lull me into something that resembles sleep. The Lieutenant continues to stare down at the floor. I know that stare well. He's dead; he just doesn't know it yet.

9.

I wake up to someone pulling my left eyelid up. I jerk forward and nearly headbutt the new person in the nose. He steps back and then resumes checking my other eye.

"Sir, we're here. Are you able to move?" asks Lieutenant Cooper from behind the new soldier.

I pull my hand up and move my head around to try and get some sense of where we are but the soldier with the flashlight keeps trying to hold my head straight. I stop and look at this new one in the eye and then bring my hand up to the pen light and grab it out of his hand.

"Sir, I need that to—"

I toss the pen light into the confines of the cockpit behind him. "I'm good," I say to the new soldier and try to give him an approximation of the stare that Scott would have given him. It works a little and he moves back for a second and then tries to check my pulse while bringing out a blood pressure cuff. I protest and wiggle in the restraints until I find the buckle of the harnesses.

The new soldier starts advising me again, "Sir, your body's been through a lot of trauma and—"

I put my arms on his shoulders and push him down to the floor and out of my way as I stand up. My body creaks and moans in places I never thought it was possible for it to make noise. My right ankle feels rubbery and, as I move to find out where I am, my left knee gives off a weird bone-on-bone pain. Breathing is also painful, but so is just standing.

"Are you rejecting medical treatment, sir?" asks the new soldier as he gets up from below me. I pull out my pack of cigarettes and light up.

"Sir, you can't smoke here. This is a—" he starts to say but I stare at him again and he shuts up.

"Where are we?" I ask Lieutenant Cooper. He moves out the open door of the helicopter and motions for me to follow him.

My entire essence protests movement. I feel like there's a micro-me inside my head screaming in pain, telling me to stop, but I push his screams into the back of my brain. I step down and out of the belly of the helicopter and see Virginia.

The sky is a yellow haze of smoke and sunlight; tiny particles fall from the sky like snow, but it's too late for snow, especially if we're in Virginia. There are mountains and some dense thickets of trees surrounding us. Buildings are designated by *Area A* signs with call numbers; there are several parking lots full of military vehicles, and some of them look like the ones that we passed by in Cleveland. Some of the transports look even worse. The entire perimeter is encircled by razor wire and three levels of chain-link fencing. Just outside the second line of fences there are smoldering piles of bodies, with three-man teams of what appear to be soldiers decked out in plastic suits with round tophat-style plastic heads. One man stands guard and the other two chuck more bodies onto the fires.

Just outside the first line of chain-link fencing, as far as the eye can see, there are monsters. I try to swivel my head around, but that's just a bad idea so I turn around slowly and take in the perimeter: monsters and bodies and fires all around.

I look over to Lieutenant Cooper, and ask, "Where are we?"

"Mount Weather, sir, or what's left of it."

I look back towards the first three-man crew and the pile of bodies and whisper, "Jesus."

The soldier that was checking my vitals exits the helicopter, pushes past us and makes his way down a massive ramp that leads into the inside of the clear-cut mountain we're standing on. Everyone else from the helicopter moves to follow after him.

"Sir, we need to move; this area isn't safe," says Lieutenant Cooper.

I don't want to move, so I light up another cigarette and offer him another one. He shakes his head and looks at me as if I don't understand English.

"Sir, did you hear me?" he asks.

I nod and look out towards the Blue Ridge Mountains, engulfed in smog and the sickening smell of burning, rotten flesh. The little particulates of ash are starting to accumulate on my shoulders and head. Ash from the piles of bodies, the smell of roasting meat, the sound of gunfire in the distance, the fences, the helicopter, everything begins to swirl. I put my hand out as if to steady myself on the helicopter but completely miss and start towards the pavement. Lieutenant Cooper catches me before my face makes contact.

He pulls me back up and stands me as upright as he can; I lean into him and we begin to walk towards the blast doors of the compound. We stop a second later when both of us realize that there seems to be an entire battalion of armed troops tensely standing in a semi-circle around one man.

Lieutenant Cooper stands up straight and nearly drops me. I can't make out the face from here, but the fact that the man is the only one standing in a suit and the Lieutenant went to attention can only mean one thing. It's McMillan.

God is a vengeful and spiteful God, indeed.

10.

The man in the suit moves towards us with purpose, taking great big strides, and closes the gap between our two positions in no time. The soldiers keep up with him and form an open perimeter, following behind them is a small camera crew.

I begin to smile as I see McMillan's familiar features moving closer towards us. Lieutenant Cooper manages to salute him with his left hand. McMillan, along with his guards and camera crew, stops a few feet from us and he returns the soldier's salute with a crisp, formal one of his own.

The reporter behind the group begins saying something into the microphone about the situation.

Robert McMillan and I stare at each other for what feels like an eternity. I can't help smiling at him. The reporter continues to talk about "how brave the President is for coming out of *Area B*." I feel the trickle of a giggle forming in my chest. It hurts.

Lieutenant Cooper addresses McMillan as "Mr. President, Sir," and McMillan addresses the Lieutenant as "soldier."

Then the Lieutenant goes on to update him on where I was, and how he found me. McMillan's eyes are wide in disbelief and hate as he looks from the Lieutenant back to me. I let out a small snort of laughter and they stop for a second and both look down at me. I hold my hand up to signal that I'm sorry. They continue to debrief each other. I start to hiccup from holding in the giggle and McMillan can't ignore me any longer.

"Do you find something funny, Mr. Sorbenstein?"

I can't help but crane my head up and look at him through my one good eye; I can't keep the smile from my face.

"I find a lot of things funny, Rob, but this…" I say and wave my free hand around the perimeter of the base and then stop on him. "This is by far the most hilarious fucking thing I have ever seen."

I felt Lieutenant Cooper tense when I called McMillan "Rob"; I saw the rest of the soldiers tighten their grips on their weapons when I waved my hand. Now I know where I stand.

"If I were you, Jeff, I wouldn't be laughing," he says.

McMillan surprises me by addressing me like we're friends again. I push off of the Lieutenant and try to stand on my own. The soldiers surrounding McMillan bring their weapons up and sight me down. He waits for a second and surveys my movements, then brings his hand up and motions for them to lower their weapons.

I try to hold my head up and scan around to the other soldiers' faces, but they are all protected by helmets and gas masks.

I stop on McMillan again, then let my head fall back down.

"You know, I half-expected to see Phil and Janet standing next to you," I say to McMillan.

I can't see his face, but I would guess by the way he shuffled his feet slightly, he didn't want to talk about that little issue.

"They didn't make it out of Cleveland."

"That's a shame," I say back and smile to the pavement.

The news reader behind the group goes on to try and punch up the tension of the situation to the camera. I bring up my hand and point to the camera and crew behind him.

"Who are you broadcasting to?"

McMillan judges my instability and then answers. "Mount Weather is home to nearly half a million people; we have a closed-circuit TV station."

I try to look up at him again, but I can barely keep my body upright so I continue to stare down at the ground. "That's impressive," I say.

"And we're going to put you on trial for your crimes against humanity," he ads.

"I've already done my time," I say back to him with a laugh.

"This isn't about time, Jeff; this is about justice," he says in the most macho bullshit way you could ever imagine. He's playing to the camera, to the people he's leading. This is a puppet show.

"So what's the verdict?" I ask, stepping further away from the Lieutenant and towards McMillan. The soldiers tense again, but McMillan motions for them to stay calm again. He takes a step forward and then stops and stands up straight.

"You're going to stand trial for the end of the world, Jeff, and everyone knows you're guilty."

I can't help but start to laugh at the words, at him and the shadow play of the moment. The laughing hurts my stomach and burns my chest. I move my free hand to massage the small of my back.

"Well, then, I guess I'm still famous," I say and manage to look at him in the face.

He looks three times as old as he did on the day that he came to threaten me in my building. His hair is nearly silver; the lines on his face are hardened and deep. As he scans me, I notice how his eyes have lost their hungry animal quality. They appear to be distant and dimming stars in the deep-set shadows of his eye sockets. He's already dead, too.

"I guess so," he says back in disgust and without missing a beat.

"Well, let's make it count, then," I say as I reach under my jacket and pull out the pistol.

McMillan's eyes go wide as I pull the trigger. The explosion of gasses from the barrel echo out into the surrounding spaces between us, the single shot comes back to me as a thunderclap from a distant storm. It was a wild shot but hits him squarely in the chest. The .40 caliber slug rips a hole into the front of his shirt and reaches all the way through his body to exit out the back in tiny fragments of tissue and a great big glob and spray of blood.

I pull the trigger again and watch as another bullet rips open the side of his face and pushes teeth and bits of jawbone up and out into the haze. Lieutenant Cooper reacts and lunges out and to the side as the rest of the soldiers pull up their rifles and sight me down.

I smile and pull the trigger one more time as the first bullets from the soldiers tear into me. The last shot hits McMillan in the gut and little pieces of his intestines protrude like baby squids from his belly as the force of the bullet dissipates into his body.

The news reader begins to scream and cry. The cameraman is steady and true, careful to keep focus on the action as it plays out, as bits of my body begin to fall away from me, as bullets from no less than fifteen assault rifles begin to slice my body in half. The pain is non-existent because the second you feel it, your brain starts to shut down. It's like little bits of electrical current in my head start to click off.

Everything grows dim, but before I pass out I see my right arm become a strand of jerky. I look down to the ground and my hand is still holding the gun. I look towards McMillan; two of the soldiers pull him back towards the blast doors. He's gurgling blood; he's leaving a skid mark as they pull him.

The news reader tries to compose herself but she can't; there are tears streaming down her face. The cameraman begins to dial in the zoom on the camera. I watch as the great eye of society pushes towards me, in a tighter and tighter shot to get the close-up.

So I smile for the camera, because I'm the man that's just shot the President of the United States, because I'm the most famous man in all of America, and because this is the end.

THIS IS THE END

ERIC POLLARINE

Eric Pollarine is an author, freelance writer, book reviewer with *flamesrising.com*, and constantly disheveled musician who lives, works, writes, smokes and drinks far too much coffee in beautiful dreary Cleveland, Ohio. You can contact the author through Facebook, Twitter, Tumblr and stay up-to-date with other goings-on, through his website *www.unlikelyconvergence.com*.

THIS IS THE END

ALSO BY ERIC POLLARINE

A Man of Letters

Stories Around The Campfire With Uncle Eric

One Fine Day
(Available late 2011 Early 2012)

Pale Horse
"The Complete Collected Stories 2011"
(Available 2012)